Reality an
inside of her.

It couldn't be possible. The odds of her getting pregnant after one sexual encounter seemed so...

Like fate.

No. She refused to believe that anything like fate was wrapped up in Romeo Accardi. Yes, it had been inevitable that they were going to do that. But inevitable that they were going to find themselves together forever?

No.

It seemed like a cruel thing that it took minutes for the test to reveal the answer. Both too short and too long.

But the two lines were inevitable. Undeniable.

She was pregnant with Romeo's baby.

Her stepbrother.

The man who hated her more than he hated just about anything else in the entire world.

That man.

She put her hand on her stomach. She was pregnant with his baby. Pregnant with his baby. It seemed laughable. It seemed ridiculous.

Books by Millie Adams

Harlequin Presents

The Forbidden Bride He Stole
Her Impossible Boss's Baby
Italian's Christmas Acquisition
His Highness's Diamond Decree
After-Hours Heir
Dragos's Broken Vows
Promoted to Boss's Wife

The Diamond Club

Greek's Forbidden Temptation

Work Wives to Billionaires' Wives

Billionaire's Bride Bargain

HEIR OF SCANDAL

MILLIE ADAMS

PRESENTS

MIX
Paper | Supporting responsible forestry
FSC® C021394
www.fsc.org

**Harlequin®
PRESENTS™**

Recycling programs for this product may not exist in your area.

ISBN-13: 978-1-335-21351-8

Heir of Scandal

Copyright © 2026 by Millie Adams

For questions and comments about the quality of this book, please contact us at CustomerService@Harlequin.com.

TM and ® are trademarks of Harlequin Enterprises ULC.

Harlequin Enterprises ULC
22 Adelaide St. West, 41st Floor
Toronto, Ontario M5H 4E3, Canada
www.Harlequin.com

HarperCollins Publishers
Macken House, 39/40 Mayor Street Upper,
Dublin 1, D01 C9W8, Ireland
www.HarperCollins.com

Printed in Lithuania

HEIR OF SCANDAL

CHAPTER ONE

HATRED WAS SUCH a fascinating sensation. It had a taste: metallic and acrid. A feeling: a heavy weight that sat at the center of her chest and made her heart beat differently. It had a scent: whiskey, spiced cologne and old leather.

At least, for Heather Gray it did.

Because hatred smelled exactly like her stepbrother, Romeo Accardi. God, she wanted nothing more than to wrap her hands around his throat and squeeze until...

If he were dead she'd never feel this way again. The idea nearly took her own breath away.

It was maybe poor taste for her to ponder his death while his father lay dying in the room upstairs. But he hadn't been sympathetic to her when her mother had passed last year and now Giuseppe was close to following his beloved wife to the afterlife and she could still hardly get a whiff of emotion from him.

Just that same spiced cologne, which for her would always create a red haze of rage.

It had always been this way.

From the moment she and her mother had darkened the door of the Accardi mansion, when her mother had been nothing but a housekeeper and Heather had been a twelve-year-old girl, awkward and uncertain, thrust into a world she didn't understand.

Because right away Giuseppe had gone out of his way to give more help than they'd ever gotten before.

Where do you plan to have the child get her education?

At the public school down the road.

Nonsense, she shall go to the same school my son attends. Fairfield is sure to give her the sort of future she deserves.

I could never afford it...

It is part of your compensation, Miss Gray.

And so Heather had gone to Fairfield, with all of the rich kids, a daisy among the hothouse flowers.

It had been a trial by fire, a strange fire she had never seen before. When her mom had taken the job at the Accardi home it had been a chance for them to try something different, to be somewhere different.

After a childhood spent in New York City, living in an apartment the size of a closet while her mother cleaned houses on the Upper East Side, her mother had longed to give her something else. A taste of another place. Of another life. Perhaps her mom just wanted a different life, and Heather couldn't fault her for that.

She'd heard about the opening through the gossip network with other cleaners—a wealthy Italian looking for a housekeeper for his property in the Italian Alps, but also for potential travel to other homes he kept around the world. The salary seemed so generous that it almost felt like a scam. Perhaps human trafficking.

Her mother had taken the risk.

The job came with a house on the estate, and for the first time in her life Heather had her own bedroom. She was still sad to leave New York. For all that they'd had very little, the city itself had a heartbeat, and it had resonated inside of Heather every time she walked to school, whenever she went to the bodega to get snacks, to find something to eat if her mother was working late.

The space and quiet of the Italian estate was deafening to her. It felt frightening. Yawning. Stranger still was the way Giuseppe Accardi treated her and her mother like they were people. He made eye contact. He spoke directly to her, not around her. Not as if she were an ornament or a pebble sitting in the middle of the floor that didn't belong.

They arrived in the summer, before school term at Fairfield started. And he had told Heather that she was allowed to use the pool.

That was the first time she saw him.

The man who would become her stepbrother.

Romeo Accardi.

Two years older than her, and already built like a man. In hindsight, she could see that wasn't strictly true, but at the time she had been…

Dazed by him.

He was six feet tall, shirtless and muscled, standing by the pool, his black hair slicked away from his face, a pair of dark glasses covering his eyes. He was the most beautiful human being that Heather had ever seen. And her mother had worked for celebrities.

She had seen her share of beautiful humans, both

on the silver screen and at her mother's cleaning jobs for the rich and lovely.

She had seen her share of glamour and glory. Somehow, even at fourteen, Romeo Accardi supplanted them all.

But everything his father was, he was not.

The first time he looked at her, he was not struck dumb as she had been when she laid eyes on him. Rather, his lip curled into a sneer.

"Who are you?"

"I… Heather. My mom works here."

"Are you meant to be at the pool?"

"Your father said that I could."

He had lowered his sunglasses, looking at her with deep disdain. "I see."

Then he had left. As if sharing the same air as her was anathema. That had set the tone.

Things did not improve after that. In fact, they only got worse when her mother began a romantic relationship with Giuseppe.

Worse still when they got married.

It wasn't a clean start to a relationship. Carla Accardi, Giuseppe's wife, had always been a distant presence in the house. At least from Heather's perspective. The beautiful, statuesque socialite hadn't been cold; she'd simply been the way that employers usually were.

When the relationship had started between Heather's mother and Romeo's father, he had been insistent his romantic relationship with his wife was long over. At least that was what he said later.

It had been confusing for thirteen-year-old Heather,

whose life had been improved in almost every way by her mother's relationship with Giuseppe.

And yet she had known that the way it had all come about was…wrong. She also had no control over any of it. Which, to this day, was the most important angle on that, she felt.

As an adult, she didn't think her mother was responsible for the dissolution of the Accardi marriage. The truth was, there had to be issues. Many of them, in order for infidelity to have been able to get a foothold. And Giuseppe wasn't a serial adulterer. He had married Lisa Gray and they had stayed together until death did them part after Lisa suffered a heart attack two years ago.

In the end, Heather saw them as a love story. An imperfect one perhaps, but over the years it had become clear that they were meant for each other. At least, it was clear to her.

One thing she could be certain of was that Romeo had never gained any perspective on the situation. As a result, Heather had never gained any perspective on him.

When his father and her mother had married, his disdain and distance had turned into outright cruelty. He blamed her mother for his own mother's unhappiness, and he hated Heather.

Popular and adored by all of their classmates, he had made her life a living hell at school. And then he had proceeded to make it hell at home as well. When he was in residence, that was. Often, he was with Carla.

But when he was around he never hesitated to make his dislike of their family situation known.

Their warfare was as covert as possible, of course. Heather would never complain and risk ruining her mother's happiness. She had never really understood why Romeo bothered to hide his disdain, but while they were never friendly to each other in any situation, they were civil—mainly—in front of their parents.

If it had changed when they were adults, Heather would've been happy to revise her opinion of him. Like her, he had been young and at the mercy of the adults in their lives. But he had never changed. He had never grown any kinder, or seemed to gain any deeper understanding of the complexity surrounding his parents' marriage or anything of the kind.

He had been just the worst. Responsible for making her life miserable.

As if her rumination had conjured him, Romeo strode into the library where Heather was sitting staring at her computer. She felt him before she saw him. That low, vibrating frequency that always resonated in her chest when he was near. And then she looked up.

He was wearing a resplendently cut navy blue suit, his dark hair pushed off of his forehead, his jaw as sharp as broken glass. The artful stubble that covered it was like a tease. As were his full lips, which looked mobile, like they might smile easily and beautifully. The truth was, they did. For other people.

Never for Heather.

That had been one of the most damaging things about Romeo back when they'd been teenagers.

He liked everyone. To know him was to long to be in his orbit. He was like the sun, creating warmth and light wherever he went.

She was the only exception.

He hated her. And when he looked at her it was like being thrown into a snowdrift.

Freezing.

But it was only one of the most damaging things about Romeo.

The other was that he was and forever, irrevocably her first experience with physical attraction.

And nothing, not the vitriol that existed between them, not the resentment that grew daily inside of her, not years or wisdom or maturity could do anything to dampen her response to him.

Hatred had a taste, a scent, a bone-deep feeling.

So, alas, did desire.

And for her the two things were intertwined in such a way that she didn't know how to separate them. She was sick.

Thankfully, after his father died they would have no further connection to each other.

What a horrible thought. That her only route to freedom was losing Giuseppe.

Giuseppe had been the only father figure Heather had ever had. He was her father.

But he had grown so frail and gray in the years since his wife had died. He had never really recovered from it. He'd gotten a cancer diagnosis afterward and hadn't seemed to have any fight in him at all. She hated to see him like this. She wanted him to be reunited with his wife. She had to believe that was what awaited him.

She wasn't looking forward to losing him. It was just that…

Finally having that last tie severed to Romeo would be a gift.

"How is he?" Sometimes if they kept the conversation limited to his father, they could make it through without having a fight.

"That eager to collect your inheritance?"

Well. Apparently that would be the case today.

"Yes, Romeo, of course that's why I'm asking about the well-being of my father."

"He is my father, Heather, not yours."

"He is my father in every way that matters. But thank you for taking this opportunity to stay in character. If we didn't have a villain in the play then this horrendous walk along the road of grief would be unbearable."

"I have never minded being the villain in your play, as you know."

"Yes. I do. You didn't answer my question."

"He's dying," Romeo said. "And nothing has on that score."

"I'll go and see him in a moment."

"What are you doing in here?"

"Sitting here counting my future riches," she said, smiling blandly at him. In truth, she had been catching up on work. She was a freelance editor contracted with several publishers, and she had a backlog of manuscripts to read and copy to write. But she had stopped trying to convince him of her goodness a long time ago.

She could remember clearly when the straw had broken her back. That very last straw. He had been on the verge of graduation, and she had been in her second year of high school. Part of his senior prank had been to get everyone in the entire school to act like she was invisible. They spent the whole day looking through her, not speaking a single word to her. Bumping into her, spilling drinks on her shoes.

Only her friend Vera had spoken to her. Well, and a handful of teachers. But even a couple of teachers had engaged in the behavior. Thus was the power of Romeo Accardi. Who had managed to frame it all as a brilliant joke, while giving her a look that told her he knew it was astronomically cruel. That it would poke at all of the insecurities inside of her. The way that she feared she would never be accepted.

That was when she had stopped. The high road had no longer been an option. Smiling at him to try to prove that she was worthy of…of something. That had ended that day.

Ever since, she had decided to give as good as she had gotten. She didn't have his power, she didn't have his influence, but in their private war she fired off as many shots as he did.

"I assume you'll be staying for the will reading after?"

She studied his face. He was beautiful. But he was empty. How could he say this, with that tone, concerning the death of his own father?

"Yes. Because it's what he wants." There was no point antagonizing him. She enjoyed it, yes, but this wasn't a game. She was about to be an orphan. And yes, she was twenty-seven, so it wasn't as if she was an orphaned child, but for the first twelve years of her life it had been her and her mother against the world. And then there had been Giuseppe. Without him, without her mom, she wouldn't be the person that she was. And whatever Romeo thought about who she was, she knew that she was a good person.

A strong one, an ambitious one. A good friend, good at her job.

Someday maybe she would actually finish writing a book, instead of just editing other people's stories. And when she did it would be because of not only the education that Giuseppe had helped her get, but also because of the confidence his love and support had instilled in her.

"What does surprise me, Heather, is that you have not found a rich man to pay your way the way that your mother did. Finding a fool like my father should be easy enough for you—you still have him convinced you're a fragile girl who needs protecting. I bet a great many men would line up for the privilege of…protecting you."

She was fed up with him. She snapped her computer shut, and stood, holding it underneath her arm. "I've been busy. Living my life. But you know, my mom didn't marry your dad until she was thirty-five. So I have time."

"Your mother pulled off a rare feat by gaining

trophy-wife status in her thirties. I wouldn't count on your charms to such a great degree."

"And what about you? Why are you here, Romeo? You have your own billions with your investment firm, and I assume you want nothing to do with your father's company. It's going to fall out of the family's hands. Publicly traded and with someone else as CEO, I assume you and I will end up with stock options. You don't need to be here for that. Are you waiting to see if you inherit this house that you hate? Are you waiting to see the last breath of a man you despise…"

"I love my father," he said. "If I despised him then all of this would be easier. Why do you think I come to holidays? Why do you think I stayed engaged in this family in any regard? You think it's because I hate him?"

That was much more complex a thought than she wanted to give Romeo credit for. She wanted him to remain the one-dimensional villain. Selfish and cruel simply because he was. She didn't want him to be someone with feelings as complicated as her own.

"I always thought it was to perform your abject disgust to all of us," she said, ignoring the revelation.

"No. I am his son. His only child. I deserved to be there. I deserved to have a place at the head of the table, just as I deserve to have my inheritance, just as I deserve to sit by my father as he takes his last breath because I am the one with the birthright to do so. You are nothing, Heather, and you never have been anything at all. He wanted your mother, and he got her. He destroyed our family in the name of satiating his lust, and then in order to save face he married his affair partner and tried to make it legitimate. If I hated him, I could've simply walked away. I could have turned my back on him and never looked at him again. I don't hate my father."

"But you hate me," she said.

"I don't see why I owe affection to a cuckoo in the nest who has spent the last fourteen years trying to supplant me."

"Maybe I just wanted a dad."

"Yours didn't want you. It didn't give you the right to mine."

Then he was the one to turn away. To leave her standing there, fuming.

She truly hated her stepbrother with all of her being.

She couldn't wait to be rid of him.

And yet she could.

Because the day she walked away from Romeo, never to see him again, was the day her family dissolved.

Then Heather would be alone in the world.

With nothing but the burning hatred she felt for Romeo remaining.

CHAPTER TWO

HATING HEATHER GRAY had become a habit.

He woke up in the morning, brushed his teeth, shaved, and he hated Heather Gray. It had been like that from the beginning.

For so long that he no longer questioned it.

He could remember the first time he'd seen her. She was sulky, insolent, the corners of her full mouth turned down. She had been a child that first time. And he had dismissed her as being unimportant, because she was.

If only he had realized that within the year she would be his stepsister. His problem.

Prior to his father destroying his mother the way that he had, he had ignored Heather when he passed her in the halls at Fairfield. But after the affair, after his mother and father had divorced, and Lisa and his father had married, it was different.

He resented her presence.

His father was enamored of her. It was clear.

His father had always wanted a daughter, and had never had one, and this was even better, because she was pathetic. She had needed saving, and his father wanted to do the saving. What better way to have someone look up at him with uncritical eyes, than to become their hero.

And it didn't matter, the ways in which he had failed Romeo and Carla. It didn't matter that he had been neglectful at best when Romeo had been a small child, wedded primarily to his business, and only later had he had any time for a wife and child. And at that point, the wife had been Lisa, and the child Heather.

In many ways, he had taken the concept of sibling rivalry with her a bit far. But he was not a man given to half measures. He never had been. His life had been his own, and then she had appeared.

He had resented her presence from the beginning, but worse was when she had become beautiful.

When her sulky mouth had become a temptation, when her body had begun to take the shape of a woman's.

She was all of the worst parts of having a sister, he assumed. And yet she wasn't his sister, and that made the entire situation abominable. It always had been.

He was surrounded by socialites who starved themselves for a living. He had always liked women in every shape, but there was a particular sort of lean, hungry look that was more popular within the circles he ran in, and Heather was an anomaly.

She wasn't polished. Even though they wore uniforms to Fairfield, she had managed to look…different. She had buttons on her backpack, and her plaid socks pulled up to her knees often had a safety pin clipped to them with things dangling from it. It was maddening and strange. Her brown hair was a curly tangle, never tamed, and she was…

Lush.

She had only grown more so.

Her hips were round, and he had thought more than once about what it would be like to grip hold of them as he drove into her. Her waist was nipped in, but there was a softness to her stomach that held his fascination. And then of course her breasts… A man could spend a lifetime on fantasies centering on her breasts.

He felt that at this point he very nearly had.

And what a thing to be thinking about as he stood in front of the door of his dying father's bedroom. His stepsister's breasts.

He couldn't wait to excise her from his life like the tumor that was currently killing his father.

He pushed the door open, and went to sit beside the bed.

"Romeo," his father said.

"Yes, Dad," he said softly in Italian. "I'm here."

He was angry at his father. He always would be. There had been a strange sort of pain that had come with Lisa's death two years ago that stilled his tongue now. She had died suddenly. She had been there, and then she had been gone.

It had been astonishingly painful, and to this day he couldn't quite articulate why. He had spent the better part of the last decade and a half hating her. For what she had done to hurt his mother, for what she had done to change his life. But she had been a lovely and loving person. She had, in some ways, been better for his father. His mother and father had a tumultuous relationship, and he could admit that there in the relative silence of his father's room. In his own mind.

Lisa and his father had never been tumultuous. There had been deep care between the two of them. He resented that too. That in many ways it was undeniable that life had been smoother for his father once he had made the decision to rid himself of his first wife.

But Romeo was the one who had to be there for his mother. Then and now. He was the one who'd had to pick up the pieces, and there were so many pieces.

"You have to take care of her," Giuseppe said, his voice thin.

"Who?"

He had been thinking of his mother, but he knew very well his father didn't care about her. He knew the answer before his father gave it.

"Heather. I need to know that she will be okay."

Of course he had no similar concerns for Romeo. Romeo had never had the option to be anything but okay. His father expected him to get on with things. To be hard. To be a man. And so he was. Self-sufficient and successful.

But what he loved about Heather was that she was soft. Bookish and in need of support.

At least that was how he saw her, but then, Giuseppe had a rescue complex, when he felt the person could be rescued. Which had left Romeo's mother on her own, and Heather and her mother well cared for.

Heather was much more canny than his father wanted to believe.

"I assume you're leaving her enough in the way of money to ensure that she's just fine."

"She needs protection. She is not from this world, and she never has been. She never fit in."

He had alienated her from any potential friendships at school. The only friend she'd had had been another girl who socialized on the periphery. He had been the most popular student, and he had wielded that social power against her.

The idea that his father would think that he would stand by and take care of her in his absence was ridiculous.

He might not be a high school bully anymore, and on some nights he could muster up a little bit of shame for his behavior then, but he was never going to take care of her.

"Father…"

Giuseppe's hand shot out, and he grabbed hold of Romeo's forearm. "You must take care of her. She's special. I love her as a daughter, and with her mother gone she will be alone in the world if she doesn't have you."

"No harm will come to her," Romeo said.

In the early days, he had fantasized about revenge. In fact, he had made her life difficult because what he had wanted was the ruin of her and her mother. He had wanted them to be unhappy in this world, miserable; he wanted it to be the cost of destroying his family.

He no longer wanted that. But he wanted nothing to do with her either.

"Promise me," his father said. "If she needs you, you will be there. Promise me that you will not abandon her. That you will maintain a connection."

He gritted his teeth, his lip curling. "I promise."

His father would be dead within the next couple of days, and he would never know what Romeo did or didn't do. He felt it was a kindness to lie to the old man now. Why give him cause for concern? But Romeo would not do the bidding of a ghost.

"Send her to me."

"Of course."

He stood, walking out of the room, anger burning in his chest.

He walked down the hall, and her bedroom door opened, and there she appeared, wearing a yellow dress that complemented her golden skin tone, the low neckline showing her curves off in a way that proved too compelling for him to ignore.

"He wants you," he said.

"Okay."

He should've just let her go on without him, but he felt compelled to follow her. He pushed the door open, and stood there as she went to his bedside and took his hand. "What is it, Papa?"

The smile on his father's face was a cold dagger pushed through his heart. And this was always and ever the problem. He could see how much more his father loved them. But in a few days this would be over, and he would go back to his life. He would go back to New York; he would take a lover for a night and blot out all of this. He worked, he played—the end. He was, in fact, an island. And the only real connection he had, the only real relationship he had to maintain, was the one with his mother. Because she needed him. She had no one else, not really.

"I love you, Heather. You are my daughter. This… this estate, I want to leave half of it to you. Because you are both my children. You…"

His anger rose up inside of him, but he said nothing.

"You don't have to do that," she said. "This estate is part of your family line."

"I will," he said. "I'm leaving it to both of you. Because I love you in equal measure."

That was like a sword straight through his chest. Perhaps it shouldn't be. This girl who had come into his life a mere fourteen years earlier mattered just as much to him as his own son. He had been right to hate her.

Always.

"I love you," Heather said.

She leaned in and kissed him on the cheek. And then he sat up. "I feel cold."

He lay back down, and then his breath left his body.

While holding Heather's hand.

It was done. His father was gone.

And it wasn't him who had been holding onto him, but his stepsister.

Who would inherit half of the estate that had been in their bloodline for hundreds of years. She had successfully supplanted him. In every way that mattered.

He had known it would be like this. From the beginning.

CHAPTER THREE

The beginning

SHE'D NEVER SEEN a boy who was so tall. Or so angry.

She'd never seen anyone like him. Not at any of the other houses her mom had cleaned in the past. But then, this place was unlike any they had ever been at.

No one had ever given them a house before. Especially not one so nice as the one they were living in now, down at the bottom of the garden of the vast estate.

And certainly no one had ever given Heather permission to use the pool.

Her mom's new boss was lovely. One of the kindest people that Heather had ever met.

And this must be his son.

Romeo Accardi.

Giuseppe had spoken about him before. She knew his name; she had simply never seen him before. He had been away on an après ski vacation with his mother, and then had gone on to the Riviera with friends. She had wondered how in the world he kept up with his school.

"Romeo is quite like his mother. He always finds a way."

It made sense, right then, as she looked up at him. She had never seen a boy that tall. A boy who was also a man. She couldn't explain that thought; she could only feel it. She waited for him to smile. She smiled, her very best, most aggressive smile. He lowered his sunglasses, and fixed her with an insolent glare. "Does your mother know that her child is loose about the premises?"

She felt like she had been cut in two with his words. With the sheer dismissiveness of them, the coldness. But also his beauty. How could anyone so beautiful exist? And how could something so beautiful be so… forbidding?

He was nothing like his father.

"I… I have permission to swim."

"It's a good thing I'm leaving then."

That was her first interaction with him.

It was a while before she had another.

Giuseppe had invited her to come into the house on the days when her mother was cleaning, and she often did. Perusing the library, or enjoying the food that the staff made for her from the kitchen. Yes, it was generous. Overly so, but she was also living in some sort of dream. Going from spending much of her day alone in an apartment in New York, walking to school and back by herself, to this.

"Have you thought about school?" Giuseppe asked.

"I've been enjoying the break," she said honestly, looking down at the tangerine she was holding, the one she had just taken out of the kitchen, as he'd given her permission to do.

"I think that you should go to the same school that Romeo attends. It is the best school in the vicinity."

"There's no way that my mother can afford that."

She already knew. That the gap separating her and Romeo Accardi was far too vast to cross. She knew. There were the people that owned these houses, and there were the people that cleaned them. And there was not enough elbow grease in the world to work yourself from the position she and her mother were in to the other. You could not start from where she did and become one of those illustrious creatures, and much of that inequality began with the education. When you were given access to the best of everything from the very beginning, how could anyone ever hope to catch up with you?

"I will pay the fees," he said.

"But why?"

He smiled. "You're smart to ask the question. There are a great many people in this world who do things for the wrong reasons. I like your mother very much. I've never met anyone quite like her. And I want to give her a gift. You are the most important thing to her. I know she'll appreciate it."

Her mother had. When he'd brought her into the room and told her how it would be, she'd been more than appreciative.

Before Heather knew it, she was being outfitted for school uniforms. The navy blue sweater with burgundy trim and plaid skirt, knee-high socks and loafers felt like something out of a television show to her. Which actually was more real than the private school kids that she had seen wandering around the Upper East Side. It was more likely for her to step into a movie than to join one of those groups.

Fairfield was in London, which put her a short plane ride away from her mother. It was foreign and exciting all at once. She'd been sorry to leave the estate in some ways, but she felt...part of something new. Part of something she'd never imagined she could be, and that made her more excited than anything.

The old building was made of stone, and more of a palace than a school. The night before school started she stayed in Giuseppe's London town house with him and her mother. Romeo did not join them. He was taking a different plane, apparently.

That sort of casual reference to their riches still astonished her.

They were astronomically wealthy, she knew. You couldn't live the life that she did and not be aware of it. But to go from their estate—in a private plane—to a glorious town house that also belonged to this family. The a luxury car and the school that was right out of a fantasy novel truly underlined the reality.

That feeling of the wealth surrounding her, compared to her own lack, followed her into the building.

She thought she would just keep quiet, do nothing to expose herself—as one of the impoverished, and as an American. She found out quickly that she wasn't the only American. The first time she saw Romeo in the hall, she heard him saying at an elevated whisper, "She's the housekeeper's daughter."

And that was when it began to follow her, like a trail of whispers. She didn't belong. Romeo did his best to make sure that everyone treated her that way. He did not manage to drive a wedge between herself and the initial friends that she met on the day, her roommates, who treated her with kindness even though Romeo was doing his best to ensure that everyone else treated her like she was invisible.

Quite literally.

Sometimes she would speak to somebody, and they would ignore her entirely.

When they went home on break things were no better. Romeo treated her like a ghost that haunted his house. Like an insignificant thing, and she hated it. She ached to matter. To be more. To not be stuck as something lower and lesser simply because she'd been born without money.

She'd always been aware of it.

Her mother cleaned for rich people; how could she not be aware of it?

But existing half in that world and half out of it was a glorious, sharp pain she'd never imagined before.

During summer break, however, she noticed that something was different between her mom and Giuseppe. They weren't like a boss and an employee.

They seemed like…friends, perhaps.

Or maybe more.

Within a year, Romeo's parents were divorced, and Giuseppe and her mother were engaged.

At fifteen, Heather was elated. It made her *one of them*, in many ways. She was no longer the cleaner's daughter. She was Giuseppe Accardi's stepdaughter. But that made Romeo her stepbrother, and if she had hoped that it might spark some sort of familial relationship between them, or even a civil one, she was disappointed.

At the wedding, she had on the most beautiful dress. It was peach colored, and finer than anything she had ever hoped to own. And he had been there, lanky and glorious in a suit cut perfectly to his lean frame. He had grown since she had met him the previous year. His face more angular, even more perfect.

His mother was a great beauty. He had his father's olive skin, black hair and dark eyes, and his fashion model mother's bone structure, her insolent mouth and the same sharp gaze. The few times that she had met the former Mrs. Accardi, Heather had felt cut to pieces by her steely blue eyes. Mainly, she hadn't lived in the house. Evidence, as far as Heather was concerned, that she could see a lot of his mother in him now.

"They might dress you up," he said, looking her up and down, and then circling her slowly, like an elegant predator. "But you will always be the housekeeper's daughter. And you will certainly never be anything to me."

It was lucky for her that she was no stranger to snobbery. Even going to the school she had, back in New York, she had been bullied. Her mother was a cleaner. And while many other kids at the school were in the same situation that she was, the ones that weren't, who still felt insignificant, thought to make themselves feel superior by creating a pariah out of someone else.

The fact that Romeo couldn't leave her alone let her know that he had a vulnerability. If he was entirely sure of himself, he wouldn't come for her. Which was what gave her the strength to simply smile in return.

Her response to him that day at the wedding only made things worse.

Soon, their rivalry at the school became quite legendary among their peers. They were smart, of course. Teachers were never the wiser, and therefore neither were their parents.

And then one thing happened that she had not seen coming at all. Her mother marrying Giuseppe really did increase her popularity. And soon it felt as if lines were drawn through their school. Who sided with Romeo, and who sided with Heather?

There were no high roads taken.

She wasn't the underdog anymore, and she refused to be treated like she was. She invited a group of friends to the house for a pool party over the summer—and given that their school was in another country, it was a weeklong affair. Having access to that sort of luxury was a dizzying drug. She had a lovely home to invite her friends back to, places for them to stay. And an indulgent stepfather who lived to make her happy, particularly since he couldn't seem to make his own son happy no matter what he did.

Heather was happy to step into the role. She'd never known her father. And Giuseppe was wonderful to her.

He wanted to spoil her, and Heather wanted to be spoiled.

The entire pool area was transformed for them. Cabana set up with lavish fruit trays, glorious flower displays, various grottoes for them to take pictures to put up on social media.

Everything was going well, until Romeo prowled to the pool area, wearing an open white shirt. At seventeen, his body was more muscular than it had been when she had first met him. She despised herself for noticing. She despised herself for still finding him beautiful at all, because certainly his behavior should have transformed him into precisely what he was. Someone who was dark and ugly on the inside. And yet he remained stubbornly beautiful.

"Good afternoon," he said, resting his forearms on the gate that separated the pool from the rest of the estate.

Her friends exchanged glances, and giggles. They knew that the official stance was that they hated Romeo, but they also weren't blind. The trouble with Romeo was that he was charming. He had a reputation for being an exceptionally good kisser, and she suspected more. Though, no one was foolish enough to breathe such a thing in front of her.

"What is it that you want?"

"Shocking, *cara*. I come to say hello and you greet me with venom."

"I don't think you find that shocking at all," she said, standing up from where she was on her lounge chair, wearing the bright pink bikini that she had just bought for the occasion. And that was when she saw it. His eyes flickered over her body, and his reaction wasn't neutral.

He had made a mistake. He had just made a mistake. He'd *noticed* her.

He noticed her body, the same way that she noticed his.

And he had let her see it.

He might hate her—she believed fully that he did—but he was not immune to her. And that was an incredibly interesting piece of information. She walked closer to him, not looking away from his gaze. "What is it exactly that you wish to offer?"

"Oh, I live to serve," he said, not breaking eye contact.

"Do you? Are you here to play the part of pool boy?"

"Oh no, *cara*, only one of us is from the servant class."

"What a pity that I will never serve you," she said.

His eyes flickered over her again. "Someday perhaps I will have you on your knees." He didn't say it loudly enough for anyone else to hear, only her. That first time he had looked at her that gaze had been lethal. Cutting. This cut her somewhere different. And didn't leave her feeling cold. Rather she felt altogether too warm.

"I think you should leave," she said.

He grinned. "If you need me to."

That left her questioning everything. Perhaps nothing that he'd said had been real, but all designed to antagonize her. But the interaction echoed inside of her.

Finally, in her senior year, she was free of him. He graduated, and went on to university, and was never at home, never at school. Being an Accardi—even if by marriage—had made her essentially the most popular girl in school. And the only regret that she had was that Romeo wasn't there to witness the ascent. And maybe that was because his absence was necessary. Without his influence, no one knew they were supposed to dislike her. They forgot. As if it had never happened.

For graduation, Giuseppe and her mom were allowing her to use their London estate for a party. The money and detail that had gone into it was extraordinary, and Heather distantly remembered the girl that she was, grateful for everything—even for a tangerine in the corner of the kitchen—and she wondered if she had lost herself somewhere. What was wrong with enjoying all of this? Surely nothing.

She did pause to feel gratitude, rather than entitlement. But the entitlement was what buoyed her, often. Because Romeo was so intent on acting like she didn't deserve it, radicalizing those around her into believing she didn't deserve it either, so she had begun to walk around with armor suggesting that she did.

But she had to remember that she wasn't one of them. Not really. Because that actually gave her an advantage over Romeo. It did. He had nothing at stake. He was cruel for the sake of it. She was fighting for a place in a life that she knew she deserved. Having Romeo away was almost enough to help her forget about him, honestly. She had actually gotten herself a date to the party. Which was something she never managed to do when Romeo was around.

She found herself obsessing about him in strange and irritating ways, and while she would never say she had a crush on him—you could not have a crush on somebody that you hated—she couldn't lie about the effects that he had on her body. She was eighteen now, and much more aware of why she couldn't take her eyes off his chest. Much more aware of what he might mean by having her on her knees. Making fun of her, no doubt, and yet it was a mental image she couldn't quite get out of her head.

He was sexy; that was the problem. And there was no denying that. Every girl thought so. It was only that he wasn't a vile, cruel monster to every girl. Only to her.

I guess that makes you special.

Well, that was the most twisted thought she'd ever had. But it didn't matter. She was with Damien tonight, and she fully intended to lose her virginity, which was a ridiculous albatross to be carrying around her neck out of high school and into university.

All she needed was a little bit of liquid courage to loosen up. Which, with the intensity of the party, didn't take long. The music was loud, the mood electric, and she was pleasantly buzzed after the first hour, which Damien seemed to notice and appreciate as her nerves faded and she became looser and more affectionate.

Soon they were kissing on the couch, and if she thought of Romeo's sensual mouth as Damien kissed his way down her collarbone, it was only because it was a habit.

After a few moments of being on display, Damien took her hand and led her up the stairs, the two of them making their way into the bedroom.

As far as exorcising demons went, she felt like she was about to do it in a big way.

Until the door to the bedroom crashed open like an entire police brigade had broken it down.

"What is going on?"

She looked up from her position on the bed to see Romeo standing there, his black hair disheveled, his face fixed into a mask of fury, his hands clenched into fists.

"What are you doing here?" she asked.

"The better question is what the hell are you doing?" She thought he was talking to her until he crossed the room, grabbed Damien by the neck and pulled him up off the bed. "She's drunk," Romeo said.

"I'm not drunk," she slurred.

"You are," he said. "She can't consent to this—you get out of here before I call the police."

"I consented," she said.

"No," Romeo said. "You're being an idiot because you're out of your head, and this party is a disaster. Clear everyone out."

"I have permission to have this party," she said.

"Because your mother is a fool and my father never tells you no. You need to be told no, Heather Gray. And I am telling you no now."

"You," she said, getting up off the bed, and trying

to insert herself between Romeo and Damien, "are a nightmare. You can't tell me that you weren't doing far worse than this when you were in school, and now you want to come here and act like an authoritarian when you've never followed a rule in your entire life. You were probably snorting cocaine off of ski bunnies' asses when you were fifteen."

"What's good for me is not good for you."

"And since when do you care what's good for me?"

"Since this asshole was about to take you when you were drunk. I care about that."

"Romeo—"

"Get out," he growled at Damien, who did not argue. Romeo towered over him, and was broader and far more muscular. The man had filled out in the past several years, leaving the rangy boy behind. He was still devastatingly beautiful, with cheeks that could cut glass, but he could no longer be called pretty. And she especially wouldn't call him that now, while she was standing there with her heart pounding hard, with fury, with embarrassment. And then he walked out of the room, leaving her alone, shouting about how the party was over.

"You *can't*!" she yelled, trailing behind him.

"I can. I came here to sleep, and I'm not doing it with this bullshit going on."

"I've been planning this party," she said. "And you don't have the right—"

But it was too late; everyone was leaving. Everyone was listening to him like his was the only voice that mattered.

"*I hate you*," she said, standing in the middle of the now-empty town house.

"Of one thing you can always be certain, *cara*," he said, moving his face close to hers, so close that she could smell him, that spicy, masculine scent, so close that she could see the dark stubble on his jawline. So close she thought about reaching out and touching him, just for a second. "I hate you too."

CHAPTER FOUR

SOMETHING HAD BROKEN inside of him that day. When he had come to the town house, looking to sleep off some of his excess, and found his stepsister, drunk, crawling all over one of the biggest assholes he'd ever known in school.

And when said asshole had led his stepsister up the stairs, he had lost it entirely.

He knew that it was perhaps as hypocritical as she said that he was breaking up a party which was tame by his standards, but he hadn't been able to allow it. Heather Gray was a thorn in his side. And the thorn had only grown more acute as she had become more beautiful. They had been cruel to each other over the years, but after that, her behavior toward him became something like psychotic. And the twisted thing was it seemed to ignite a spark within him. Seemed to make him all the more interested in continuing the war that they'd been engaged in for years. Though they saw each other less frequently, it still happened on occasion that they would find themselves at his father's home in Italy at the same time.

Even their parents had to take notice of the rift,

though they thought it was some form of sibling rivalry rather than the burning hatred that existed in them both. They traded barbs in front of both Lisa and Giuseppe, but were careful to walk the line.

In university, Heather traded her school uniform, and out-of-school bikinis, for something a bit more serious. Her red hair was often pinned up into a bun, her color palette ranging from black to darker black.

He would be lying if he said he didn't miss the color.

But she was clearly now obsessed with being taken seriously, in that way first-year university students often were.

Which was why he had thought—the first time—that perhaps some of her anger at him might've cooled. Until she walked by him in the hallway, and looked up at him, her green eyes catching him so hard that he froze.

Then she put her fingertip on his chest, dragged it right across the front of his cashmere sweater. "How nice to see you, brother dearest."

There was malice and promise in those words, and he would be damned if they didn't send a sharp signal of arousal straight down to his cock. The problem with Heather was that she took desire and added something more potent to it. It was the extreme distaste he had for her that seemed to add adrenaline to the attraction. What was forbidden to him? Nothing. Nothing but the stepsister he hated. He was a wealthy man, and doors flew open for him. But not her. Touching her would cause an avalanche of destruction. It was what made her compelling.

Over dinner she smiled at him sweetly. Later he cornered her. "And what is your game?"

"I don't have a game," she said, smiling sweetly at him.

He'd never once seen the look on her face before.

"I don't believe you."

She pouted. "What a terrible view you have of women."

"Only of you, *cara*."

For some reason that only made her smile more.

"You need to be nicer to Heather," his father said to him later when they were drinking cognac by the fire.

"Why exactly?" he asked, tapping his glass.

"Because I won't be around forever. You will have to take care of Heather and Lisa."

"Father, your money will take care of them well enough."

"Is that all you think I offer them?"

It was certainly why they had so happily broken up Giuseppe's marriage. Certainly why they had taken to all of this with such ease. Had his father been a poor man, it would never have happened. He knew that for certain. One of the truly difficult things was that Lisa was a kind woman. Caring and one who seemed to enjoy spending time with her husband, doting on her daughter. In spite of the frosty reception that Romeo had given her, Lisa had been persistently kind to him. But he was the one who'd had to be there for his mother. He was the one who had—

"Don't forget that I have to take care of your former wife."

"Romeo... You know I feel sorry for the timing of everything."

"Not so sorry that you didn't do exactly what you wanted to anyway."

By the time he was ready for bed he was furious. He walked into his room and stripped his jacket off, his tie, the rest of his clothes. He walked into the shower and stood blindly beneath the hot spray, then dried himself and walked back into the bedroom. He stopped. There was someone in his bed. He flicked the lights on, and there she was, the covers pulled up past her breasts, her copper hair spread out on the pillow.

His stepsister was naked in his bed.

"What are you playing at?" he asked, fury and desire creating a potent cocktail in his veins.

"'Wherefore art thou, Romeo?'" she asked, that same smile from earlier today playing across her lips.

Whatever she was doing, it was evil. It had nothing to do with wanting him; that was certain.

"Get out of here, you little slut," he snarled.

"I don't think that's what you want," she said, completely undeterred by his insult.

"It *is* what I want."

His heart was racing, his body hard, and the towel that was riding low on his hips was probably doing little to disguise the effect she had on him. But no matter how much he wanted her in that moment, he wanted her out of his room more.

She began to sit up, and in one fluid movement he went over to the bed, grabbed the edge of the blanket and pulled it around to the other side of her quickly, baring her body only for a moment without looking before he swaddled her, then grabbed the corners of the blanket and carried her, trapped inside, out into the hallway.

"Out," he said, dumping her onto the floor.

She was seething, her eyes shooting sparks from where she was lying, still trapped in the blanket. "Don't you want to take my virginity? Since you spoiled my attempts the last time?"

"You were drunk," he said, staring down at her in her glorious state. "And what you do with your virginity is none of my concern. Whatever trap this is, you're not going to catch me in it." And then it all became abundantly clear. He had always known what she was, from the beginning. It was only his attraction to her that had clouded things, for just a moment. He began to laugh. "You are trying to trap me, aren't you? It is not enough that your mother married my father—do you think that you can snare me in the same sort of fashion?"

Her face turned red.

"How *dare* you?"

"How dare *you*. But you did. Now there you are naked in the hallway, thwarted. Go to hell, Heather."

He shut the door violently on her and locked it. And then he went straight back into the shower and stood beneath the cold spray, cursing her name the entire time.

Heather was lost in a spiral of self-loathing. He had *rejected* her.

She had intended him to. Sort of. She pushed her fingers through her hair and pulled hard.

Everything was tangled up. She had gotten a little bit wine drunk and told her new friends in college all about her relationship with her stepbrother, and they had suggested that half the problem was that they wanted to bang each other. She denied it for a while, but then gave up. Because the truth was, he was beautiful. And she had never been immune. She also knew that he wasn't immune to her.

"You need to screw him," her roommate had said. "It's that simple. The two of you are drowning in all your unresolved sexual tension."

And the more she had thought about it, the more she had thought that perhaps she did. God knew that her attempts at dating were entirely thwarted because every time she kissed a man she remembered Romeo storming in like an avenging angel, and it never got any further because he had destroyed the idea of sex for her. She had gotten it into her head that at the very least she would shock him. That she would get some kind of advantage over him. And if they did have sex… maybe it would defuse everything between them. But he had dumped her out into the hall, and truly, she had realized that she had miscalculated anyway. Because the feelings had been far too intense. They had been so much more than she had anticipated. And now she was humiliated.

At least no one had seen her scrabbling back to her room with his blankets. It really was too bad that he was a billionaire, because her stealing his blankets might have been an inconvenience to him if he were a normal man. But alas, Romeo had everything he could possibly want.

Thankfully, she was heading back to school tomorrow. Thankfully, she probably wasn't going to have to face him again. They avoided each other well enough in the giant house.

Usually, the only time she had to see him was at family dinner, and as much as it pained her to skip one with her parents, she would just claim that she was tired and avoid tonight.

She would be heading back to school with her tail between her legs to an extent but...

She had certainly affected him.

Her attraction to him had always been so buffered by how much she hated him, and then she had been naked in his bed and he had walked in wearing only a towel, and nothing had been theoretical about that.

She had been so sure that she would have control over everything, because she was a woman and therefore more likely to keep her wits about her during sex.

She had lost her head completely. In that moment when he had walked over there and she had thought that he...

She let out a breath, and walked out of her room, needing lunch, and needing to sneak it back to her room as quickly as possible to minimize her chances of having to deal with Romeo.

And then suddenly, she found herself being maneuvered against the wall, and there he was, all six foot four inches of her outraged stepbrother, staring at her with fire emanating from his eyes.

He was so close she could feel the heat radiating from his body. So close she could smell his scent. Again.

She swallowed hard, and he lifted his hand and wrapped it around her neck, gently, but enough to let her know that he was dangerous. That he could do whatever he wanted right then. Whatever he wanted. Strangle her, kiss her, she wasn't sure that she would stop him either way. And the realization was terrifying. It all crystallized. That first moment he had ever spoken to her, and it had been like being sliced into, the second time when it had felt that much more intimate, that much deeper. This time, she felt it between her legs. This time, it had formed perfectly into exactly what it had always promised to be. It was real, deep, adult desire mixed with resentment and rage cultivated over the course of years. She had no control. She had been wrong. She had played with this man, and she had only played herself. If he wanted to take her right there against the wall where anyone could walk by, she would let him. And that was the realization that finally made her move.

As soon as she did, he released his hold on her, proving that he had never held her so tightly as it felt like he had. "Don't play with me," he said.

She caught her breath. "Maybe we should call a truce."

"You would like that. We are not in school anymore, and I have no investments in this game. But if you think that ignoring you means that I no longer hate you, I wish you to comfort yourself with the fact that I still do. Forever."

"Same," she said.

She didn't stay for dinner. She made arrangements to change the flight plan for her father's private plane and left an hour later. With the inescapable, lowering realization that Romeo might have actually won.

CHAPTER FIVE

Now

HEATHER WAS EXHAUSTED from crying. It had been a devastating night. Losing Giuseppe had been inevitable, but she hadn't really been prepared for it. How could you prepare to lose a parent? She had now done it in two very different ways. Sudden and expected. She couldn't recommend either one.

The funeral had been planned and coordinated, and executed within a day. She and Romeo hadn't had to do anything.

Nothing but try to figure out how to go on with the pain of losing their father.

Whatever Romeo thought of her, of her mother, it didn't matter. Giuseppe was her father in every way that mattered. Losing him left a void she didn't think could ever be filled.

Losing him was losing her last connection to the Accardi name. To the illusion she'd ever been part of the family. For her it wasn't about assets.

She wasn't even sure when the will reading was happening and the specter of it was filling her with anxiety every time she took a breath. Giuseppe had said she got half the estate. Romeo wouldn't be happy. An understatement, and who knew what other surprises the will would have?

In the meantime, Heather had been fielding phone calls, managing things that she would have expected Romeo to do, but he was remote and even more unfriendly than ever.

She couldn't wait to be rid of him.

Dealing with him was the bane of her existence. The scourge of her life.

Every embarrassing, humiliating, terrible thing that had happened to her had him tangled up in it. She just…despised him.

Complicating her grief and turning it into an endless tangle of anger on top of everything else.

Things had changed in the years since that last, explosive confrontation between the two of them. They had changed the way they dealt with each other. She had gone back to university after that failed, utterly ill-advised seduction attempt, and thrown herself into her studies. She had changed the sort of people she hung around with. Had switched her major from hospitality to English, and begun pushing toward a career in teaching, which had then shifted to publishing. And which was currently freelance, which gave her an ample amount of freedom, freedom that she knew had only come from the relative privilege she had started out with.

She was the daughter of a cleaner. And the world had opened up to her when her mother had married a wealthy man. She had gotten lost in private school games for a while. She liked to think that she had found a piece of herself from before, and done good work integrating it with the woman that she had become, discarding some parts, clinging to others. She liked to think that she had become a better person. Though whenever she was around Romeo she didn't feel like a better person. And currently, she didn't feel better at all.

The doorbell rang, and she went to answer it, not waiting for a member of staff.

She knew the man at the door. Gray haired and serious, it was Marcus Santos, Giuseppe's attorney.

It was time. The clock was ticking. The will.

"Hello, Mr. Santos."

"I'm very sorry to hear about your father."

Heather nodded. "Me too."

"I've come to read the will. He left me strict instructions to do it as quickly as possible because he was worried that things would become acrimonious between yourself and…" His sentence trailed off, his eyes traveling to a place behind Heather. And she knew why. She felt Romeo's presence without having to turn around.

"My father's will?"

"Yes," Marcus said.

"He was afraid that there would be an uprising if it wasn't read immediately?"

"Yes, Mr. Accardi," Marcus said, never looking away from Romeo. "He was."

Normally, Heather would've enjoyed watching

somebody stand up to Romeo, but her chest still felt like a hollow cavity. Enjoyment was a distant thought.

They went with the attorney into the dining room. They sat at the table, and he read out very plainly the terms of the will. Romeo's mother was to get a stipend, relatively limited, but certainly enough. And the rest was to be split evenly between Romeo and herself. Including Accardi Industries.

"That's outrageous," Romeo said. "Heather is not part of the day-to-day running of the company."

"This is not up for debate."

"She was an *English major*," Romeo said, with the same disdainful tone he might have used if he'd called her a garbage collector.

"These are the terms of the will," the lawyer said.

"You got your way," Romeo said.

"I don't want it," Heather said, seeing it as simply another chain tying her to him.

"Will you sign it over to me?"

"Yes," she said. "For the monetary value."

"Then it will be done."

It was a double-edged sword. Trading the Accardi legacy for money meant severing ties she valued but...

She wanted to be free of him. She *needed* to be free of him.

She wanted to have no association with him whatsoever, and being part owner in a company with him was not the way to do that. But she could feel his rage. She knew where it came from. It was because his father had seen them as equal. Because he had given her exactly what he had given to Romeo, and Romeo felt entitled to more. To everything.

"All of the assets are to be divided evenly."

"Good," said Romeo. "We will liquidate it all. Everything other than the company, and we will split it. You see to that. I don't want to see her again. Not after today."

"You think I want to see you?"

"It's hard to tell with you."

"Then let me make it explicit," she said, holding up her middle finger.

"Do I need to send a police escort to get one of you away from the property?" Marcus asked.

"*No*," Romeo said. "Leave us."

"Yes," Heather agreed, her pulse pounding. "Leave us."

Marcus did, even if grudgingly. He kept looking back like he might have to suddenly intervene in a fistfight.

Romeo moved to the double doors of the dining room and closed them in a fluid motion.

"It is settled," he said. "I'll buy you out. We liquidate everything. We are not family. The Accardi empire is mine. The Accardi name is mine. It isn't yours, and it never has been. My father is nothing more than a deluded, sentimental old man who believed that a gold digger—"

"My mother was not a gold digger, and you know it. Your mother is a gold digger, one who is being taken care of, even after your father's death. You could be angry that they had an affair. I can understand that, but the love story, in the end, was your father and my mother, and that is not ambiguous. Your mother is a selfish, awful woman who has spent years making sure that you don't get to enjoy your life because you have to do her bidding." She'd seen the way he acted whenever Carla called or texted. The way he responded to her marching orders, abandoned holidays and family dinners and meetings to go to her.

His eyes were like black holes, filled with fire and loathing. "How dare you! How dare you speak to me like this! Of such things, when you came in here with nothing and are leaving with everything all because your mother was a homewrecker."

"The home was already wrecked, Romeo, be realistic. My mother was not responsible for the state of your parents' marriage."

"It is a good thing I am no longer responsible for you."

"You never were. You've never been responsible for me. What you have been is a vengeful, diabolical, seething..." She realized then that she was moving closer to him, and he to her.

"And you are nothing but a brat. The moment that you had access to money and to wealth, what did you become? No better than me, so you cannot claim a high road where we are concerned. You are a grasping, manipulative..."

And then, suddenly they were so close they were sharing the same air.

"I hate you," she said.

"No more than I hate you." Then he wrapped his

arm around her waist and brought her body up against his. "And we never have to see each other again. Not after today."

Adrenaline coursed through her, excitement lighting her up. She could feel a pulse beginning to beat between her legs.

It reminded her of that night in the hallway when he had grabbed her throat. Of the night before that when she had climbed into his bed and he had come out of the shower naked.

But this time there would be no consequences. No consequences because they never had to see each other again. There would be no holidays. No family summers, no more dinners.

She would be free of him once and for all. He lifted his hand and traced her cheek with his knuckles. "I can think of no more fitting goodbye," he said, his voice low.

"Yes," she said, her body feeling like a stranger's now. She was driven. A need, and not a lovely, romantic desire, but this toxic, utterly forbidden desire she had always felt for her stepbrother.

Part of being free of him would be to have this.

She knew it. She had always known it. Even though her attempt at seducing him had been half thought out, and all the way stupid all those years ago, it had come from a place of realizing that a powder keg packed this tightly would always be a risk. It had to explode.

It had to.

With them, it might be murder, or it would have to be sex.

She would take the sex.

He reached his hand back, and grabbed a fistful of her hair, drawing her head back, exposing her neck, and then he lowered his head and kissed her.

Right there, where her pulse was beating at the base of her throat.

She let out a raw, completely unhinged cry of pleasure.

She had expected that the first thing he would do was kiss her mouth, but no, he trailed hot, violent kisses up her neck until he reached her lips, and then he consumed her. His mouth bruising, his tongue taking no prisoners as he plunged deep into her mouth. She began to tear at his clothes, his tie, as he began to remove her clothes from her body.

"You will no longer have any power over me," he panted as he tore her shirt away from her body, then popped her bra open at the front, filling his hands with her breasts before lowering his head and licking her nipples, pressing her breasts together so that he could devote attention to both, then sucking her hard until it hurt. She didn't feel any sort of hesitation. She didn't feel any hint of virginal nerves. This was how she knew absolutely and completely that Romeo Accardi had broken her long ago. Because this was what she had always craved. The violence of it. The darkness.

Nothing else had ever been able to compare. Why would she want candlelight and roses when she could have this?

This man who despised her so much, shaking as he rubbed his thumbs over her slick, tight nipples. As he had to inhabit his own despised desire for her. As he surrendered to it. Yes, they were both consumed with the sickness they shared, and that made it something glorious.

She was disgusted with herself. And yet that guilt, the shame only made it hotter.

It only made it that much more intense. And they had been building on this intensity for more than a decade.

Every barb, every cruel comment, every moment where they had undermined one another, every time they had played with one another, it had been leading to this. The most twisted foreplay, and it had brought them here.

She popped the buttons off his shirt and pulled it away from him. Finally she was touching this body. He had taunted her with it for years, and finally it was hers.

It was her turn to lick him, dragging her tongue over his nipples, over his muscles, his chest hair.

"You're starving for me," he said, his face set into a sneer.

She nodded, and began to work his belt free.

"I knew I would see you on your knees for me one day, Heather. And now here you are, begging. Starving for it, aren't you?"

Where was her pride?

It was gone. He would be the one begging later—she would be sure of it—but for now it was her turn, and she would accept it. She would revel in the humiliation, because it was hers and hers alone. Because this was their great and terrible shame, and so while they could dole it out to one another, they would also both have to live fully in the consequences of it.

She let him guide her down to her knees as he opened the closure on his pants. As he let his hard cock free, the sight of him, a sight she had only been teased with before, that night when he had been wearing a towel and she had seen that he was hard for her, made her mouth water.

"You always have so much to say. Perhaps you will find your mouth better occupied now."

He thrust his hips forward, pressing the head of his arousal to her lips, and she took him in greedily, the first taste of him on her tongue sending her off into a spiral. She choked on him, gladly. Took him in as deeply as possible as he thrust his hips in time with the movements, touching the back of her throat.

And then he pulled himself away from her, his hand shaking, for all her shame. Because she might be the one on her knees, but he was the one on edge. She wiped the tears off her cheeks and stood up slowly, unzipping her skirt and kicking it away, slipping her panties off and being careful not to catch the fine lace fabric on her high heel. She had on nothing but those shoes, and the long pearl necklace she put on this morning. She lifted the necklace up and caught it between her teeth, watching as color mounted in his face. All the muscles in his body tense, on red alert.

"You're begging to be fucked," he said.

"And you're begging to fuck me."

He growled, and closed the distance between them,

lifting her up and laying her down across the long table. That site of all those family dinners. And here it was, this perfect mockery of the familial connection that they had never been able to feel. Only hatred, mingled with extreme desire. Extreme need. All of it playing out now, in the most decadent way. Then he pulled her up to the edge of the table, lowered himself to his knees and buried his face between her legs. It was not a slow seduction. He began to consume her. Like all the hunger, all the anger of the past decade had suddenly burst inside of him, leaving him feral. He pushed two fingers inside of her, the stretching feeling making her gasp as he thrust deep and hard, his tongue playing over her clit as he tormented her. As he pushed the desire up to unbearable heights in her body. Until her orgasm broke over her like a wave, and she cried out his name, leaving deep grooves in his shoulders with her nails.

And that was fitting. Because that was the way it was between them. So much pain, so much need. The pleasure was blinding, though the cost seemed worth it. So very worth it.

"I need you," he ground out, climbing up onto the table, and kissing her mouth, letting her taste evidence of her own arousal as he hooked her leg up over his hip and thrust deep inside of her with no quarter.

This was not making love.

But she had never believed that they would.

The need was far too sharp, far too intense. He claimed her, the brutality of it beautiful, at least to her. She was lost in it. Everything they were. In everything happening. The glide of his cock inside of her, this closeness that felt far more like torture than intimacy of any kind.

And when she came again, it was like she had gone somewhere else. Years and years of pent-up need all folding in on itself and taking her somewhere beyond her body.

He gripped her hips, his hold bruising as he came hard, spilling himself deep inside of her, the hot pulsing setting off another aftershock in her own body.

It was like a storm had passed through, passed through them, passed through the room. It was like everything she had ever wanted, and ever feared, had come to pass all in one moment. It was done. They were done.

She could finally breathe again. It was like she had exorcised the demon that had been inside of her for the last thirteen years. And now it was gone. Everything was gone. She could go on with her life; she could go on.

"I'm going to pack my things," she said, sitting up on the table, still naked, resting on her forearms.

He was already up, pushing his black hair back into place, looking remote and untouchable, as though he hadn't just been inside of her.

"No need to hurry."

"There is," she said. "There's no need for us to see each other again."

His eyes locked on hers. "No. There isn't."

She wondered then, what she was supposed to say. *Goodbye* felt like such a whimper after all that roar.

Bland and meaningless. So she said nothing. She got dressed, while he stood there watching her as he had always done. With that vague air of distaste. That superiority.

He wasn't better than her. He had been a slave to the exact same feelings that she was. He wasn't better.

She wasn't great.

But at least it was finally over.

When she stepped outside she felt like she had been thrown back in time. To the first moment she had ever gone to the estate. She felt like a child. Confused, out of place. Like all those years hadn't happened. A sob rose in her throat. But then instead of giving in, she took a breath. And another. And another.

There had been life before all of this, before him.

There would be life after too.

CHAPTER SIX

HEATHER WAS HAVING so much time trouble concentrating on her work she was starting to worry that she was going to have to tell her author that she couldn't meet the time frame she had promised to get her notes back by.

She had felt so gray and awful ever since leaving the estate. And having all of the monetary things filtered through lawyers wasn't helping the way she had thought that it would. Because it felt impersonal and terrible, and she felt like she had been turned inside out. It was all evidence of just how much awfulness had passed between her and Romeo, and…

Her body couldn't forget. She kept herself awake all night, every night, reliving what had passed between them, and then in the morning she was exhausted, sick to her stomach.

The grief mixed with all of this was just too much to bear.

She was grateful that she was doing mainly remote work, but she also sort of wished that she did go into an office every day, because at least she would be forced to get dressed and interact with people. This was all virtual meetings and chats, and it made it far too easy for her to disguise that she was unraveling.

The missed deadlines would definitely betray her.

Her stomach lurched.

She just felt...

Not like herself. She was an orphan now. That was kind of a terrible realization. She knew that when you were an adult nobody thought of it that way, that's how it felt. Drifting and rootless.

She had thought that cutting ties with Romeo would feel like a triumph.

She had thought that maybe she would go on dates. Be a normal person.

Right after it had happened, when she was on an adrenaline high she had called Catherine, her roommate from college, and she had told her that she had finally gotten her stepbrother out of her system.

"Well, thank God," she said. "Now maybe you can have a functional relationship with a nice man who doesn't want to degrade you while he has sex with you."

Catherine had been joking, but then it had forced Heather to reflect on the fact that she and Romeo had gotten a fair amount of pleasure out of degrading each other. And then that had sent her into a spiral where she had spent the entire night replaying what had happened. The most intense, soul-searing moment of her entire life.

Why were things so complicated with him? It didn't make any sense. It should just be nothing. Especially after all that.

She put her glasses back on and tried to focus on her reading, and her stomach turned.

She felt so nauseous and gross this morning. For a while she had been blaming that on her lack of sleep. She always felt gross when she didn't sleep. But it felt more pronounced now, out of the vague nausea territory and into something a lot more...frightening.

She took a breath, and stood up, trying to stretch and ease the unsettled feeling in her stomach.

A message popped up on her computer, not in her office interface, but from Catherine.

You've been very quiet, and I'm starting to think I need to send someone after you.

I'm fine.

Are you?

Feeling a little bit sick today, actually. But I've been feeling rough the last month and a ½.

It's to be expected, I guess.

I guess.

Suddenly, she felt like she was about to lose her breakfast, such as it was, and she ran into the bathroom, where she cast up her coffee and biscotti.

She went back to her messages.

A little bit worse off than I thought, since I'm vomiting up my coffee, which I need to survive.

There was a long time between that message and a response.

I feel like this is a stupid question, but there's no chance that you're pregnant?

Heather stared at the message. And stared and stared.

There had never before in her entire life been a chance that she could be pregnant. Everything that had happened had cast such a haze over her that she hadn't been thinking clearly. She had been so busy cataloging how fuzzy her brain was that she hadn't thought at all about her cycle. She also hadn't thought about…

They hadn't used a condom.

She had felt so raw, so exposed, so stripped bare by the entire thing that she hadn't given that enough thought. Hadn't done anything in the aftermath to prevent pregnancy.

"Oh my God," she said. Out loud into the silence of the room.

Are you pregnant?

The question flashed up on the screen, and then her phone rang. She picked it up. "I don't know," Heather said, because she knew exactly what Catherine was about to do, and that was ask the same question again, but this time verbally.

"You need to get a test."

"It can't be… We only did it the one time."

"Surely you paid better attention in health class than that. Your education was really expensive."

"I know," Heather snapped. "But it's just… That can't be. I'm never supposed to have to deal with that man again."

"Did you use a condom when you had sex with that man?"

"No," she said.

"Heather…"

"I know."

"You can still… I know it's not ideal, and I know it's nothing that you would've planned, but you don't have to be connected to him if you don't want to be."

She sat with that, for a very long moment. And Catherine just let her. In the silence, in the reality of it all.

"I can't not tell him," she said.

"Why not? He's awful to you."

"I know that. I know that, but his father was so wonderful to me. He changed my entire life. And…" She swallowed hard. "My mom was a single mom. It was us against the world, and I'm alone."

"You're not alone. You have me."

"I know that. I'm extraordinarily grateful for it. But the truth is, I was just sitting here feeling so incredibly sad. My mother worked so hard in order to support us, and I don't even have to worry about that. I'm working because I choose to. My stepfather just…died and made me a multimillionaire, which isn't even fair. But it's the way that it is. It's what happened. I don't have any excuse for not taking care of the child, and if it wasn't Romeo it would be straightforward. I would just keep the baby and never tell the father. But he's going to know."

"You don't even know yet," Catherine said. "Have somebody go get you a pregnancy test. You're rich."

"I don't even have to be rich to do that—there are apps for that."

"Well. Send somebody."

So she did. And she waited. And waited. She and Catherine were messaging now instead of talking on the phone, as she paced around waiting for the test. Reality and denial were warring inside of her. It couldn't be possible. The odds of her getting pregnant after one sexual encounter seemed so…

Like fate.

No. She refused to believe that anything like fate was wrapped up in Romeo Accardi. Yes, it had been inevitable that they were going to do that. But inevitable that they were going to find themselves together forever?

No.

Then on top of that she had to contend with the fact that she might become a mother. That didn't scare her. That would actually make her happy. If it weren't for Romeo. He was the wild card. He was the problem.

The doorbell rang and she nearly jumped out of her skin. She buzzed the courier up to her floor, and they left the package outside. She waited for them to leave, then opened it up and took hold of the bag. With shaking hands she discarded the bag onto the floor, and began to unwrap the test on her way into the bathroom, leaving a trail of trash behind her. She read the instructions carefully—she had never even seen one of these out of the box in person before—and followed those instructions as carefully as possible. It seemed like a cruel thing that it took minutes for the test to reveal the answer. Both too short and too long.

But the two lines were inevitable. Undeniable.

She was pregnant with Romeo's baby.

Her stepbrother.

The man who hated her more than he hated just about anything else in the entire world.

That man.

She put her hand on her stomach. She was pregnant with his baby. Pregnant with his baby. It seemed laughable. It seemed ridiculous.

She called Catherine.

"It was positive."

"Do you want to change your mind? Because I will fly there immediately. I'll give you whatever you need. I'll help you."

"I'm not changing my mind. If there's one thing I've never been it's afraid of him. I'm not scared of him now. It's just…exhausting."

"Of course it is."

"You think I'm crazy."

"It's not up to me. You and he have some kind of connection that I can't understand. I've never met the guy, but I've seen pictures of him. I understand why you're attracted to him, but he's awful to you. I've never understood why you… You have feelings for him, Heather. That's always been obvious. He's half of what you talk about in any given conversation."

"My feelings for him are toxic and negative."

"I think you wish they were. Only that. Anyway, let me know how he reacts."

"I'm going to have to get on a plane. I can't tell him over the phone." Just thinking about it made her laugh. "I've never spoken to him on the phone. Of all the ridiculous things. But why would I? We don't like each other. We don't talk to each other. This is ridiculous."

"I agree. It's ridiculous. But you have to deal with him in the way that only you can."

So she did one of the first very rich person things she had ever done as a woman who'd gotten a substantial inheritance. She booked a charter on a private jet. And then she cried the entire way to Italy.

CHAPTER SEVEN

ROMEO WAS EXHAUSTED. Talking his mother down from her latest episode had been worse than any business negotiation he had dealt with. Sometimes he wondered if this was his life. Forever. Always flying across the world to where she was when she told him that she didn't want to live anymore. But what else could he do? She was his last remaining parent. His father had done terrible damage to her, and she had never recovered. She was always seeking to re-create that relationship with new men, new lovers, and it was never good. It was always toxic. And it was just...

On top of that he was still dealing with Heather. Still dividing up all of these assets to liquidate, working on the legal aspect of buying her out of his father's company. Her lawyers were being nitpicky with details, and he was about to...

He thought of her. Every night. And those thoughts left him hard and aching, and he couldn't even bring himself to go out and find another lover because she had haunted his libido in such a way that he couldn't exorcize the specter of her.

Every time he looked at another woman he saw her.

He had gone through bouts of this for a good portion of the last decade. But never this strong. Now he knew what it was like. To taste her. To be inside of her.

He wanted to get drunk.

That was his singular goal as soon as he walked into his father's old home. Everything was boxed up, ready to sell. Except for what had been his father's office, and the bedroom that Romeo used. Also, that damned dining table was still sitting there. The scene of the crime.

He was filled with hate.

Right when he walked through the front door, he was confronted by his own personal ghost.

There she was, her hands clasped in front of her, her face white.

"What the hell are you doing here?"

"It's both of ours," she said.

"I'm well aware. But I thought that there was an implied agreement that I would handle all of this and you would simply take the money."

"There may have been that agreement. But things have changed."

"Why? Or did you decide you wanted more?"

Something sharp flashed in her eyes. "And what if I have? What if I decided that I want what's rightfully mine? To be part of this family, because I am. I am part of it. And you can resent me all you want, but your father saw me as a daughter. You've been trying to supplant me—"

"Don't do this. Not now. You never wanted to see me again, and yet here you are."

"Because things are complicated now," she said.

He saw tears in her eyes, the sloped set of her shoulders, the pale color in her face, and that was the first time he felt truly disquieted.

Because there was one thing that Heather had never shown him, and that was weakness. She was weak now—he could see it—but what he didn't know was why.

"What is it?"

"I've got to tell you something."

She sounded grave. Grave enough that he wondered if she was telling him that she had poisoned his father. Or something similar.

"What is it?"

"I..."

"Dear God, Heather, you have never had trouble telling me anything difficult. Hard truths are in fact your favorite thing to speak to me, so just go ahead and say it."

"I'm pregnant. With your baby, obviously."

It was like the world was crumbling and falling away. Pregnant? With his child? How could that be? How was it possible?

You know perfectly well how it's possible.

He had taken her like a rutting animal; he had taken no precautions whatsoever. He had assumed that she had taken some. Well, that was a lie. He hadn't assumed anything. He hadn't thought about it. Never in his life had he ever taken a woman without protection, and now not only had he done it, but he hadn't even been aware of it. He had been aware of nothing at the time other than his need to take her. Nothing other than the triumph of finally having her.

"It's impossible."

"I thought the same thing, but tests don't lie."

"You will be getting another test, one that I can see."

"Why would I lie about this? You would find out. I'm not an idiot. You're a very rich man, I know how paternity tests work. There's no way and no point to be lying about this, Romeo, none at all. I wanted to be free of you. This is the last thing that I want."

"Then why are you here at all? If you want to be free of me."

Panic was tearing through him, and he felt wounded; he felt the urge to wound her back, as he had always done. And in the back of his mind was the realization that this was going to send his mother to an extremely dark place. A child with the daughter of the woman who had caused her so much pain?

This was untenable.

It was unimaginable.

"I can raise the child by myself. But if I do that, you can't be involved at all. You can't claim them. You can't… There is no middle ground when it comes to this baby, Romeo. There can't be."

He stared at her, and he couldn't even begin to describe the feeling that was flooding him. The intense possessiveness, the anger. "I would never deny my own child."

His own distance from his father echoed inside of him now. The sense of rejection. He would never, ever consign a child to such a feeling. What a horrendous thought. What an evil thing to suggest.

"You know how we are," she said. Her teeth were

chattering now, and she looked sick. "We spent years living to hurt each other. When we are left to our own devices the choices we make are poor. There have to be…protections. Rules. If you want to be in this child's life, we have to get married."

"You dare come in here and make demands of me? Prove correct the thing I thought about you all those years ago? You were trying to get me to impregnate you then, weren't you? I always suspected it."

"No," she said, vehemently. "And I don't need you to. I was left just as much as you. This has nothing to do with trying to get anything, but it has everything to do with being the child that was always on the outside. Think about it. This child would never truly belong if we didn't get married. I would marry someone else, give the child some siblings, and they would only be half of that family. You would do the same. Who would that child belong to? And what would happen to them? I know what it's like. I loved your father so much, Romeo, and you never accepted me. You made me feel like I was an outsider all of my life, and I will not allow it."

"Why do you think you're in a position to allow anything? One way or the other. Why do you think—"

"If you don't agree, then I will fight you with all of my resources, and I will paint a picture of you that isn't flattering at all."

"And what will that do to our child?"

"You have choices, Romeo, you just don't like them."

"What will a marriage look like between the two of

us? We can't even be in the same room without wanting to kill each other."

"I know. It's terrible. An awful situation and a terrible idea. But from where I'm sitting we don't have
another choice. We need to do what we must for this
child."

"So for eighteen years you expect us to live in a
prison cell with one another?"

The truth was, he would've demanded marriage. He
would have. Because he would not allow any child of
his to be born and stigmatized the way that she was. He
had been part of that stigma. He knew it. He couldn't
deny it. And he had seen how cruel the other children
could be. Even when she had been the stepdaughter,
they had whispered behind her back. She had friends,
plenty of them.

But…

The trouble was, she was scratching the surface of
the deep truth.

A child who was the product of a union between
stepsiblings who had a reputation for long hating each
other was going to face extreme ostracization. And it
would be only their fault. They would've created the
situation. And so it was up to them to mitigate the
damage. He had already lived thirteen years of hell
where Heather was concerned. What were eighteen
more years of it?

It nearly made him laugh. They both thought that
they were going to be free.

And yet, when had he ever been free? He had been

thinking about her constantly since that moment. He had been obsessed with her.

For so much longer even than the last month and a half.

"We will have to construct a narrative," he said. "One of romance."

"Why?"

"You're thinking about our child, and that I find admirable. In some ways. But what you're forgetting is the fact that you and I have a reputation for hating each other. It is well known. Particularly in the circles that I'm in. Not unknown in yours. If you want to nip gossip in the bud, then it must... There must be a story. It can't be that we hate-fucked on the dining room table."

Her face turned red, and he felt his own body go warm in response to mentioning what had happened between them.

"I guess. I guess you're right. And what will our marriage look like?"

"I don't know," he said, and nothing pained him more than admitting that he didn't have an instant, immediate plan. It was infuriating, in fact, but there was no roadmap for this. He was a man who was accustomed to control, but with her, he was always out of it.

With her, everything was always near destruction.

"We will have to draw up paperwork. Very clearly defined paperwork."

"It's almost as if you don't trust me."

"I don't. You spent years making my life miserable, Romeo. You deliberately hurt me from the moment that I first came into your life, and you can blame the fact that our parents had an affair. That hurt your mother, but you were mean to me from the moment that we met. Nothing more than a snob. The thing that you now realize you have to protect your child from is you."

Her words lanced him through the heart.

"You grew up without a father," he said. "And your pain is that of a stepchild. I understand that. My pain comes from growing up in a war zone. And having to deal with the consequences of the fallout when that war zone exploded. I have just come from talking my mother down off a ledge, quite literally. She is mentally fragile. And I am the only one that bears the burden of caring for her. If you marry me, then you will assume part of that burden."

He didn't know why he said that. Maybe because he wanted her to feel the weight of it. He knew that he could trust no one but himself with his mother's care.

No one knew the extent of it, but she'd begged him to never tell. Why give Giuseppe the satisfaction of knowing he'd hurt his ex-wife's mental health this way? Why tell anyone when it was something he could bear alone?

"I… I'm sorry. Though I doubt that your mother wants anything to do with me."

"She won't have a choice. You're going to be my wife. The mother of my child."

The words tasted acidic on his tongue. How could this be happening?

They both stood there, with unspoken truths pulsing between them. He could ask her to terminate. He could say that he didn't want anything to do with her and the child. Neither thing was a real option in his mind. He had lost his father. And this was a link to him in some ways. It was carrying on what had been ended.

Perhaps if his father hadn't only recently died he would make a different decision. He wouldn't feel so compelled to do this. But he did now. He did now.

"We will have our lawyers draw up paperwork for the marriage. Detailed prenuptial agreements, and conduct requirements."

"Oh, that sounds lovely."

"You and I both know that we can't be trusted."

She blinked. "No. I don't suppose we can be."

"Obviously now the sale of the estate will not go forward," he said.

She bit her lower lip.

"What?" he asked.

"I moved back to New York for my job. I don't see myself living here."

"We will split the time between the two, but this place is now the legacy of our child."

"Now that there's a baby we're not burning it to the ground anymore?"

He chuckled. "We lost that privilege."

"I don't understand any of this. It's like no matter how hard I try to get away from you there is a rope that keeps pulling me back."

"It might be a tripwire," he said.

They were silent for a long moment. "I didn't do this on purpose. The idea that I could've planned it… It's ridiculous."

The vulnerability in her words stopped him. Shamed

him. He did tend to see her as a character. A viper spitting venom. A creature, rather than a whole human being. But here she was now, a woman pregnant with his baby. She was not simply...

He had built her up in his mind. His enemy, for all intents and purposes.

"What was the purpose of you coming into my room all those years ago?" It had always astonished him that she had done that.

"To seduce you," she said. "Only when I got there did I realize that I was in over my head."

"You wanted to seduce me? Even then?"

"You're not a fool, Romeo, you know what happened between us to create this situation. Do you think that it just appeared there? It didn't. You know that."

"But even then..."

"I told my roommate Catherine about you. She said it sounded like we needed to work it out of our systems. I agreed then. Except I was a virgin and... Your anger was more comfortable than the other things that I felt."

"You were far too young to feel something like that."

He didn't know why he needed to resist that.

"I was eighteen. I knew what I wanted, but I didn't. It's different now. That's why it happened. I knew what I wanted."

"Some sexual experience taught you the extent of your feelings, I assume?"

She laughed and looked away from him. "No. Does that make you feel good, Romeo? You got my virginity after all."

Shock tore through him. It had never occurred to

him that she could've possibly been a virgin, not with the way that they had attacked each other. Not with the intensity of the encounter. Or the skill with which she had tormented his body.

"Impossible."

"You are so arrogant," she said. "You think that you know me. You think that you know me better than I know myself? You think that you know me better than all the evidence around you. You just think that you know. Back then I was somehow grasping and greedy enough to try to seduce you, while also knowing that I had stolen your father from you. That I wouldn't need anything from you because I had so effectively cut my way into his affections that I would be getting the lion's share of the inheritance anyway. And now you think you know more about my body than I do? You bursting in and ruining what was supposed to be my first time actually caused emotional damage."

"I should've let that drunken frat boy have his way with you? I'm not the villain in that story—that clumsy, grasping bastard is the villain. I saved you."

"Why?"

"Because it was the decent thing to do. Because I wanted you for myself. Do you have any idea the manner of torture that you have meted out to me for the past ten-plus years? I have been in hell. You appeared and turned my entire life upside down, and then you had the audacity to be beautiful with it."

He was breathing heavily, his heart raging.

"And this is exactly why we have to make legal deals," she said, moving away from him. He could see the pupils in her eyes dilate, darken. She wanted him. Just as he wanted her. Even now. Even as they were facing down the prospect of having a child. Having to deal with each other for the rest of their lives because they would always be linked. Now, they would always be family. The thing that they were running from they had inadvertently run toward.

Or perhaps it hadn't been an accident. It was so difficult to say with her. Always.

"The truth is," she said quietly, "you don't know me. Maybe you have wanted me all this time, but that doesn't mean that you know me. I am a creation of your imagination, and very little else."

"And does that mean that you can accept that perhaps I'm the same to you?"

"You've been cruel to me."

"As you have been to me."

He let out a long, slow breath. "I will have the estate put back in order. Go back to New York, and get everything sorted that you need sorted. My lawyer will be in contact with yours and we will begin drawing up the prenuptial agreement. There will also be a separate contract regarding expected spousal behavior."

"Oh, how lovely."

"You of course are free to revise it and add what you would like."

"Fantastic."

"The final revision will be done in person. I will require your presence back here. You will live here primarily for the duration of the pregnancy, I assume that you can arrange remote work with limited time in the office?"

She looked filled with spite. "Yes. I can."

"Good. Let us start this off on the right foot, and not in opposition to one another."

"I'm happy to do that, but that doesn't mean letting you be in charge of everything."

"Of course not."

"You say that, but I don't trust you."

He tightened his jaw, looked at her. "Perhaps we must start trusting one another."

She met his eyes, the gold in them fiery. "Trust has to be earned."

CHAPTER EIGHT

THE FIRST COPY of the contract came through while Heather was in the middle of meeting with client to arrange her time away. She wasn't able to look at it until she was in a car headed back to her apartment. By the time she was upstairs in her room she was fuming. She forwarded the contract to her lawyer along with a screed of notes that she trusted her to turn into a coherent revision.

Then she called Romeo. A video call so that he could see the anger in her eyes, because why miss out on that opportunity?

But as ever, she wasn't prepared for the impact of him. Why was he still beautiful to her? After everything.

You're jumping headlong into a marriage with this man. What do you think that's going to look like?

That was the scary thing. It was difficult to say what a marriage to that man would look like. Very difficult indeed. And yet she didn't see another option.

"I assume that you got the paperwork?"

"This is patriarchal nonsense," she said.

"What exactly?"

"Well, particularly the control that you're asking to have over my sex life."

"If you're unfaithful to me I will take you for everything that you have," he said.

Rage flashed through her. "And you?"

"You're welcome to submit a return argument."

"So I have to live like a nun or I have you as my only option?"

He was wearing a black suit. His black tie was slightly loose, and his hair was disheveled. It made her wonder if he had been with someone else. Even now.

Thinking of him that way... It made her so angry. It also sent a shiver of desire through her body.

"The question I have for you," he said, his gaze meeting her directly through the camera lens, "is if you think we can live in close quarters without touching each other."

"I am willing to try. Also, expect my response soon." She hung up the call, and paced around her apartment before stripping off all her clothes and getting in the shower, turning it on cold. The thing was, she had suggested marriage thinking about the baby, and really not about them. In her head she had thought that maybe they could live separate lives, but have some kind of protection. Not be in real relationships with anyone else, maybe, but...

Maybe she had thought they could live like they always had. Like stepsiblings raising a baby together while he independently conducted his affairs and she worked on figuring out who else she could possibly have an affair with.

He was trying to claim ownership of her. But did that mean that he wanted her? And why did that make her feel special? And not outraged?

She sent her lawyer four more emails of suggested addendums after she got out of the shower, and then waited for the response.

It went on like that for six weeks. While she wrapped everything up in New York, went to the doctor to judge the viability of the pregnancy—why go through all this if there was no baby?—threw up daily and arranged to have her mail forwarded.

They hadn't spoken in that time. It was all lawyers, but he'd insisted they meet in person to go over the final draft.

He had asked that she meet him at his office in London, before they would go back to Italy together. She hadn't been to the office in years. Not since her step-father was in charge. Romeo had acquired the company to function beneath his own luxury travel conglomerate six years earlier, with the blessing of his father. In preparation for the day when he would have ultimate ownership. She could actually understand why he was angry that she had been given half of the control.

Romeo had used his connections, his education and his personal knowledge of the industry to begin his own company that didn't work in direct competition with his father, but rather complemented it. He had started an airline, and later a multitude of cruise lines. From luxury yacht travel to large, affordable cruise ships. Meanwhile his father owned one of the largest hotel chains in the world. Now they were all under one umbrella, and Romeo was certainly more qualified to attend to any of that than she was.

She didn't even want it. There was a reason that she had ended up ditching her degree in publicity. She had decided that she wasn't going to pursue a place in the Accardi business empire.

She loved books. All kinds. When she'd been younger it had been escapism while she'd waited out long hours with her mother cleaning, and then when she'd been older it had made the situation with Romeo manageable, in a strange way. She read all kinds of books—horror, thrillers, romance, mysteries. It made her think of herself as a heroine and him as her antagonist; it made her feel brave.

Plus, she had her stepfather's money to keep her from penury, which she'd found was a big asset in publishing. It was a passion job, more than it was a job for the money.

It was also funny now, because she and Romeo were enmeshed. Deeper than her owning part of the company could ever make her.

She took the high-speed elevator up to the top floor, and didn't find Romeo in his office. She got a text directing her to the boardroom down the hall.

The room was completely private, no windows on the door. She swallowed hard, and then walked in.

There might not be any windows out into the office, but the entire exterior wall was glass, offering a view of the streets below. They were more than forty floors up, so she knew that while she had a view of the world, the world did not have a view of them.

Her heart felt like it was being squeeze by a giant fist.

He wasn't in there yet. She had a feeling that was by design. She sat down at the head of the table. That would make him angry.

She despised herself with a little thrill of adrenaline that raced through her at the thought of making him angry. She got off on that. She was going to have to work on that, probably.

The door opened, and there he was. All in black, looking sharply pressed. His gaze flicked to where she sat, and then he walked down the length of the table, taking his seat completely opposite her.

He got out his briefcase, the sound of the locks being opened loud in the relatively quiet room. He took out a stack of papers and tapped the edges once on the edge of the table with a crack, and then slid them across toward her.

"This is where we're at," he said, indicating the contract.

He had left it deliberately out of her reach. She stood up and walked to the center of the table, suddenly aware that the V-neck on her shirt was quite low. When she bent down to grab the papers, she watched his gaze, noticed the way that he looked at her cleavage.

The power play aroused her, and she had not come here to be turned on.

But then, she supposed if she didn't want to be

turned on she shouldn't consent to share the same air as Romeo.

She began to look down the prenuptial agreement. If either of them broke the stipulations of the agreement, the other one would be given full custody, and a sizable share of the other's assets. They had both agreed to that. They had both agreed that the shackles needed to be tight, because what made sense now might become difficult for them to abide by in the future.

But when she reached the part about marital conduct, she stopped. That had been the most contentious part. Because what they had agreed was that either they had no control over each other's sexual conduct, or all of it. The current version of the contract said that all extramarital sexual encounters had to be consented to by those within the marriage. And that there would be consequences if the affair ever became public.

She looked up at him. "I think that this covers everything."

"I have added another page," he said.

"Have you?"

"Yes. For you and I to go over and make adjustments to." He took a pen out of his briefcase and clicked the top once.

She turned the page. There were addendums to what she had previously seen.

In the event that both parties decide to conduct a sexual relationship with each other then sex outside the marriage becomes unacceptable.

She looked up at him. "You think that's going to happen?"

"Keep reading."

Provided that the sexual relationship is satisfying to both parties. Wherein all kinks and desires should be catered to and orgasm shall be achieved by both.

Her face went hot. "All kinks?"

"Why take anything off the table before you've tried it?"

Was he trying to goad her? Make her run? Make her freak out?

Oh, please, asshole. We've been at this for too long.

Her heart was beating rapidly, her face hot, and she took her own pen out and made an amendment to kinks, and to the section about orgasms. She slid the paperwork across the table to him. His dark eyebrows raised high. "Two orgasms to every one of mine?"

She threw the pen down and leaned back in her chair. "Women are multi-orgasmic, Romeo. If you're not up to overachieving, certainly I can find someone who is."

"Oh, you misunderstand me. The only question is why stop at two?"

Her throat went tight. "I assume we'll be busy sometimes."

He looked back down. "I think you might want to leave some of these things on the table."

"I don't need you to *spank* me."

"Don't you? Sometimes it seems as if you're asking for punishment."

"Not interested," she said, her heart beating faster, her pulse beating rapidly at the base of her throat, calling her a liar. Oh no. She was lying. His eyes continued to meet hers as he pushed the contract back toward the center of the table. She went and retrieved it. She crossed out the part she had added about spankings, bondage and other forms of submission. But her pride wouldn't let her leave it at that.

And so she took it upon herself to add a new section.

She passed the paper back to the middle of the table. Made him stand up, and walk over to the center of the table, where she watched him closely, every line in his body, the way that the suit fitted him. He slid the paper back with him, back to his seat at the table. He read what she had written and looked up at her. "You want me to beg?"

She nodded. "Yes. I will require begging. For what you want."

His lips curved into a smile. "And praise."

"Seems fitting."

"I thought so. That is of course, if we decide to pursue a sexual relationship inside marriage."

"Yes," he said. "Inside marriage. That is precisely what the paperwork covers."

That hung heavily between them.

After they got married, if they were to touch each other then the agreement changed. Then it became all of these paragraphs, all of these amendments. Punishment and begging.

But if they didn't touch each other then they were free to pursue other parties.

But all of that was only when they were married. It wasn't now.

Crucially. It wasn't now.

He stood up, and began to walk toward her, loosening his tie as he did so, and then, shocking her entirely, he began to slowly lower himself to his knees in front of her. He put his hands on her thighs, and began to push her skirt up her hips.

Electricity struck her, like a wave. Her heart was pounding so hard she thought she might sit. Except…

She was hot. Dizzy. Desperate.

"Is this what you had in mind?"

She had on thigh-high pantyhose—because she couldn't stand full-on types; it wasn't because she was trying to be sexy—but he lowered his head and licked the place where the lace met her skin.

She gripped the edge of her chair, watching her stepbrother's face as his tongue glided over her skin.

She gasped when he reached up, gripped her panties and pulled them to the side, exposing her as he pressed her legs wider, and dragged his tongue through her slick folds. The light shone bright through that window, and she felt scalded by it. So connected to what was happening. To the fact that it was him between her legs. This was happening again.

But it was okay. Because they had paperwork, but they hadn't signed it yet. It was okay, because it was paperwork meant for after they got married, and they weren't married yet.

Later. Later they could practice keeping their hands off of each other. Later, they would focus entirely on their child. Later.

But right now she was desperate for him. Right now, he was pleasuring her with such intensity that she didn't think she would ever recover from it. He sucked her deep into his mouth as he pushed two fingers inside of her and brought her closer and closer to the edge. It was happening so embarrassingly fast. She couldn't have resisted him if she wanted to. It was like it was inevitable. When the wave crashed over her, she cried out his name. And when he looked up at her, there was a satisfied smile on his face. "There was one."

Then he lifted her up out of the chair, brought her down on the boardroom table. Funny that it was the second time she had had sex, and also the second time on a table. Well, maybe there would be something funny about it later. Right now, she was just desperate. Tearing at his clothes and trying to get his skin underneath her hands. She tore his tie off, tore his shirt open and pressed her palms against his ridged abdomen. He was unbuckling his pants, as quickly as possible, freeing himself and thrusting deep inside of her as he unbuttoned her shirt so that he could palm her breasts.

It was completely savage and lacking in finesse. It was wild and hard. It was wonderful.

She cried out his name right before he lost control, and the two of them went over the cliff together.

His forehead was pressed against hers. "There. You

had two to my one. I'm already practicing keeping your commandments."

She couldn't believe it happened again. Except of course it had. If they could think about it, they wouldn't be in this place. If they could control themselves, they wouldn't have been here to begin with.

Now that they had acknowledged it, now that they'd done the paperwork, it seemed like there was no more restraint left.

She looked at the paperwork sitting there at his end of the table. They would sign that, and she had a feeling there was almost no point pretending that it wouldn't end up here again. But those amendments wouldn't matter. But maybe they...

Maybe she could find someone else. Maybe this was just the discovery of sex. As she lay there on the glossy boardroom table, with that place between her legs still throbbing, it felt entirely disingenuous. But she wanted to hope that it was possible. Wanted to believe that it could be true.

But then the obverse would also be true. He would have other women.

And just the thought of that made her feel violent.

"You look angry. Which is not unusual when you are around me, but it is unusual for a woman I've just thoroughly ravished."

"I'm just thinking about logistics," she said, getting up off the table and putting herself back in order as he did the same.

"Then I didn't do my job correctly."

"You did just fine. It's only that we find ourselves in an extraordinary situation."

"Is there any chance you'll ever speak to me like I'm a human being?"

The question, asked with such gravity and sincerity, shocked her. She met his gaze. "I…didn't think you wanted that."

"It isn't a matter of wanting—it seems that it would be a better way for us to be."

"We have a zero percent success rate not shagging each other's brains out when a table is near recently, and I'm not really sure what to do with that. So being human or not human is sort of the least of my worries right now."

"Understandable."

She had the sudden, disorienting thought that they had done absolutely everything backward. She hated him, down to the very marrow of her bones, but it didn't even come from a deeply realized place. She had sex with him, but she didn't really know him. They had negotiated this entire marriage on paper. She understood why they needed it. She had even been part of insisting on it. But they had always had something between them. Whether it was the baggage of what had happened in his parents' marriage, or the reality of their relationship because of their parents' marriage. Now the baby. She didn't know what it was like if they were just Heather and Romeo. She had no idea at all.

He looked…not softer now, but perhaps a little bit more human. His hair was a mess now, his tie loose…

"When I called you, you hadn't just had sex with another woman, had you?"

"Excuse me."

"Did you? Because you looked a lot like this."

"I haven't touched anyone since you and I were together. How could you think that I would?"

"I don't know you. And even more crucially, I have no reason to believe that what happened between us meant anything to you."

He moved over to the boardroom table again, and rested his knuckles on the top of it. He looked down at the surface of the table. And then up at her. "What happened between us was more than ten years in the making. What happened between us stole my ability to think critically. And I am not a man who— Of course you don't even know that. Because you think of me as someone who is driven by emotion, because when I'm around you it is nothing but sparks and anger, but that is not how I am in my life."

Well, that didn't fit her narrative and she didn't like it at all.

"How would I ever know that?" she sputtered.

"You wouldn't," he said. "You would never know. Just as I know nothing of you other than your petulance, your vindictiveness. Your…softness when you are naked. The way that you taste."

It made her want to kiss him. There had been no kissing this time. Funny how they fell upon each other with such ferocity, but didn't engage in any of the tenderness. Or perhaps not funny at all.

She moved to the end of the table, and grabbed hold

of the nearest pen, signing the paperwork with a flourish. "This agreement suits me. I will honor it. Down to every last detail."

"I sense a caveat in there."

"I think that we need to get to know each other. I think that we should practice abstinence while we... get to know one another."

"Excellent. I propose we get to know one another after we announce the engagement."

With that, he walked back to his briefcase, and took out a ring box. He held his hand out, and she went and took it from him. She opened the box slowly, and examined the ring inside. "It was your mother's," he said.

The realization of that hit her square in the chest. "My mother's."

Of course she hadn't had it all this time, because Giuseppe had kept it. She hadn't even thought of it in the aftermath of his death. "Will you wear it?"

It felt like such a double-edged sword coming from him, because he had never warmed to her mother, and had never accepted the relationship between her and his father. And yet for her it held great significant meaning. For her, it mattered.

She took the ring out of the box and slipped it on. "Thank you," she said.

She decided that she was going to take it the way that it had meaning for her, rather than the way it had meeting for him.

He was silent for a moment. "Your mother was very kind to me," he said. "Almost unfailingly. When I was not kind in return."

There was something so heavy about the admission. An olive branch that she hadn't seen coming.

"She thought you were a very brilliant mind."

She had been kind to Romeo, but she had concerns about his strained relationship with Heather. But he was Giuseppe's son, and even if he was difficult, her mom had felt affection for him because she loved Giuseppe so much.

"Thank you," he said. He looked like he was about to say something else, when his phone rang and he grabbed it quickly. His brow creased as he answered. "Yes?"

He spoke in German, quickly and decisively, and she had no idea what he was saying. There was a placating edge to his tone.

When he hung up, he looked like a haunted man. "I am going to have to fly to Vienna to see my mother."

"Oh. Is she…unwell?"

"She often is. I told you, there've been mental health issues. Ongoing for years. I am going to have to tell her about our engagement, she is already in a bad place."

"Would it help if I went?"

He considered that for a moment. "I… I don't know."

"What if I went with you," she said, looking to offer an olive branch that was in a similar vein to the one that he had extended to her. If there was one thing that was true about them both, it was that they both loved their mothers. Very much. They both could relate to each other in that way.

"You can come with me if you like. I will…evaluate the situation and see if I want your intervention."

She nodded. "That's fair."

It felt strange, to come to an agreement with him. While the touch of his body still echoed inside of her. While all the lingering memories of every poisonous and terrible thing they had ever said to each other hung between them. While the knowledge that she was pregnant with his baby settled over her.

He packed everything up, and they walked out of the boardroom. She felt disoriented now, getting to the elevator. A wave of sadness washed over her as it began to descend. "I miss your dad," she said.

"So do I," he returned.

She looked at him out of the corner of her eye. Shock weighing heavy at the center of her stomach. "I didn't think that you…"

"You didn't think that I love my father?"

"You were angry at him. Most of the time."

"Yes. I was. He distanced himself from me."

"You distance yourself from him," she said. "You were so angry after the divorce and—"

"Yes. I was a teenager when it happened."

That realization rocked her. Because of course he was. He was a child. He reacted like a child. Most of the interactions that she had had with him that been toxic and soul searing and affecting had been when he was an angry teenage boy. She had also been a teenager, so she hadn't handled any of it all that well.

But the stunning, jarring revelation that any strained relationship that had remained had probably been due in large part to Giuseppe letting a teenage boy's reaction to something dictate the whole rest of his relationship with his son was… It was painful.

"I think he believed that you hated him," she said. She felt honor bound to defend her stepfather.

"I'm sure he did. You were also completely uncritical of him, and I imagine that was a much more satisfying relationship."

"That isn't the only reason that he cared about me."

Romeo frowned. "Of course not. Of course it's not the only reason he cared about you, but you can see that it would be more rewarding to have a relationship with a child that thinks you're a superhero, versus a relationship with one who sees you as a man who could do nothing right. And for that, I carry fault. I am sorry my father and I did not get to mend that."

Of course, they hadn't been entirely estranged; she knew that. They had still seen each other at holidays, and he had often been there just to visit. But you could feel the strain in the relationship, and of course Romeo's relationship with Heather's mother had never been easy.

And now both of them were gone, which meant that all that was left was regret over what might've been. What could have potentially been if things had been different. If he had handled things differently. If his father had.

"I'm sorry," she said. "Of course you were a teenager. Of course that should've been handled differently."

"Family is complicated," he said.

Particularly theirs.

"Well, the hope is that we make ours a little less complicated."

"We're stepsiblings getting married and having a baby. I don't think there's anything less complicated about that."

"You don't already have a wife." She said that dryly, but she wondered if he'd be offended. Judging by the hollow laugh he gave in response, he wasn't.

"There is that."

They didn't continue the conversation until they got on his private plane. Which was of course the most luxurious aircraft she'd ever been on. But that was what he did.

"This is extraordinary. Did you design it?"

"I had a hand in it," he said.

"More than just a nepo baby."

"Thank you," he said, pouring himself a glass of Scotch. She was instantly envious that she could not do the same.

"Somehow I don't feel like you're actually thanking me."

"Maybe I am. Maybe you need to start taking what I say at face value."

"Maybe," she said.

"Here we are, almost getting along."

"Almost."

"I'm going to take you to my favorite hotel in Vienna, and I will leave you there while I speak to my mother. I need to tell her that you're having a baby. I need to tell her that we're getting married. I will have to get my read on the situation."

"I can't apologize to you for our parents having an affair."

He looked at her, his expression intense, a muscle ticking in his jaw. "I never expected you to."

"You blamed me for it, at least in part. Somewhere, deep inside of yourself, you did."

"I suppose. You were emblematic of what had changed. And again, I was a teenage boy. I don't…"

"You were," she said. "But later you were a grown man who continued to hate me."

"I did decide that you had tried to trap me when you were in my bed all those years ago."

"Is that really why you hated me?"

He took a long sip of his Scotch. He rested his arms on the soft leather chair he was sitting in, his legs wide. It was an obscenely masculine posture, and she regretted that she found it so attractive. She regretted that she found him so attractive. But then, that was the story of her life. Rage at Romeo, fantasize about Romeo, repeat. Forever.

"I was angry at myself. For wanting you. It's like I always knew that the consequences would be heavy. Here we are."

Was that true? Had there always been this between them? The potential for this life-altering event, had it always been somewhat inevitable?

"I hated you because you were mean to me," she said, looking out the window as the plane reached its soaring altitude.

"Now, I don't believe that. I was mean to you, but you felt something else too."

"Do you know why I was a virgin?"

"No. Because I don't know anything about you, not functionally."

"It's because you messed my sexuality up. I'm convinced of it. I trained myself to want this disdainful, awful man, who promised pain as much as he did pleasure, and I have never been able to figure out how to want someone else. Someone who's nice to me. Someone who wants my company. I want you. And that is a truly disturbing fact. I met you too soon. You shaped my sexuality, and I think you might've broken it."

She felt exposed by that, but then she'd given herself to him on a table, so what was exposing at this point?

He smiled. Slowly. "Feels good, though. Doesn't it?"

She laughed. "Yes. It does. That's how I got myself pregnant. Why are you being a a pain when I can't drink?"

"I am very sorry."

"Somehow I don't think so."

The two of them decided to do work for the rest of the flight, and didn't carry on a conversation, and when they arrived at the hotel in Vienna, she was delighted by how glorious it was. Heather had gotten used to luxury. It was part of being an Accardi. But that didn't mean she didn't find it delightful in about a hundred different ways whenever she got to experience it.

The old, historic building with its palatial interior was a sight to behold. And the penthouse room that they were in had fabulously Baroque furnishings. It was all over-the-top and utterly ostentatious, and she adored it. She walked into one of the bedrooms, and her breath was taken away by the sight of the blue canopy bed. "This place is fantastic."

"I'm glad you enjoy it," he said. "And now I have to go. I am sending a dress for you to wear to dinner tonight."

"When did you decide that?"

"During the plane ride. Tonight we will go out. Since we're doing things out of order. I thought we might want to go on our first date."

CHAPTER NINE

"WHAT IS IT that has you upset?" Romeo asked, when he arrived at his mother's bedside. It was never a good sign when she wasn't getting out of bed.

"I feel like I haven't had the chance to properly grieve your father. Because I don't hate him. I love him. He was the love of my life."

Romeo clenched the back of his teeth together. It was difficult when she was like this, because it wasn't true. He knew that. She had hated his father for more years than she had ever loved him. But now that he was dead she was wailing as if they had been lovers only yesterday.

He wanted to get back to Heather. And that was a strange thought indeed. She had been beautiful on the plane. And his body still echoed with the satisfaction of their earlier coupling.

He wanted her again. Tonight in that suite. And he knew that she wouldn't resist him. Of course she would.

She wanted this as badly as he did. They wanted each other equally.

"It just feels pointless going on. All of these years

without him have been like wandering in a desert and there is no more purpose."

"I do have good news for you," he said.

She looked at him, her eyes filled with tears. "What is it?"

"You're going to be a grandmother."

Just like that, it was as if a light had turned on; the sun shone upon her. He got an adrenaline rush, a fiery, intense feeling that he only ever caught otherwise when he was closing a business deal. A sense of triumph. Of winning. He had found the magic combination to fixing her this time. This was how it always was. She was devastated. And only he could fix it.

He had fixed it. Now he just had to break the news to her that Heather was the mother.

Because of course his mom had hated Lisa more than just about anything. That she had been left for a housemaid, one who was inferior to her in every way, had been galling for her self-esteem, and he truly did believe that she had been heartbroken on top of it.

She had carried ill will for Lisa all these years.

It was one reason that Romeo had never been able to find a way to have a good relationship with his stepmother, even though, the truth was, she had been a kind woman.

Even though, he knew, his father had had a more peaceful life with Lisa that he ever would have with Carla.

"Yes. And I'm getting married."

"That is wonderful news," she said. "You must have a big fabulous wedding. And you should do green. I look wonderful in green, and the mother-of-the-bride dress will be stunning."

"Yes. Of course there will be a big wedding. One fit for our family."

"You will get married in Vienna, not in Italy."

"There is no reason we can't have the wedding in Vienna."

It was beautiful here. And it would make a fine venue for a wedding. He could see no reason that Heather would object to the idea. They had enough money to fly all the guests here. And besides, he owned an airline.

"And who is she?"

And this was where it would be difficult. "Heather. Gray."

The shock on his mother's face nearly blotted out the earlier win.

"I am sorry if you find that difficult. I found it surprising. But…"

"You love her?"

He didn't know what the right answer was here. Couldn't quite grasp what she was looking for.

"Of course I do. I wouldn't marry her if I didn't."

She nodded. "Of course. There is something about those women, I suppose. Something about them that is quite irresistible."

"I don't know about that. But in the grief over the last few years, Heather and I found ourselves bonding."

He was lying. But if it smoothed things over, then so be it. It wasn't a problem. It needed smoothing over. "I'm pleased about the baby," she said. "A darling little child, one that I can dress up and hold and… That is good news."

She was trying to rally; he could see it.

When she was happy, she was the loveliest woman in the world. The most fun. She could be a great mother.

She could also be the most cutting, vindictive person that Romeo had ever known, and it was difficult to know which version of her he was going to get.

But he had taken it on. Because no one else had.

She was his responsibility, because she didn't have anyone else. His reward was those happy moments.

"I would like to bring Heather by tomorrow for a visit. You two can discuss the wedding."

"I suppose she has changed since she was the house-keeper's daughter."

"Yes, Mother. It's been quite a few years since you've seen her."

"Tea. Yes. That will be good."

"Yes, it will."

His driver took him back to the hotel, and when he walked through the door of the room, he was greeted by Heather, standing there in the brilliant, emerald-green dress he had sent to the suite.

"You look beautiful," he said.

It was freeing, to say that. To simply admit that he found her to be stunning. To have there be no subtext, no other meaning or emotion behind the words.

She was beautiful.

Her cheeks turned pink, and the pleasure that he saw there on her face ignited something inside of him.

"Really?"

"Yes."

He held his arm out, and she took it, tentatively. Slowly.

"How was your conversation with your mother?"

"It was good. Overall. She's happy about the baby. I made arrangements for us to have a visit with her tomorrow."

"Good," she said. "That will be...good."

"She wants for us to have the wedding in Vienna."

"Oh. Well, that's fine, I suppose."

"Thank you. I know you probably barely remember her."

They got in the elevator, and rode it down to the lobby. They walked through the ornate, gold space, and through the gold revolving door out to the street, where his car waited for them.

He held the door open for her, then got into the driver's seat. Tonight, he preferred to be behind the wheel.

"Yes, I think I was away most of the time they were still married. And she was often gone."

"Yes. I do know that my parents had marital problems before your mother arrived. I told you, I lived in a war zone. And that is one thing that I won't accept for our child. Whatever differences we have, we cannot tear each other down in front of our children."

"I agree."

"And we can never make it our child's job to build this back up."

"I agree with that too. I suspect your father wanted you to build him back up, and as much as I love him, that's not fair."

He hadn't even been thinking of his father. But he supposed in a way that was true. He hadn't reached out, had never asked his father to do it, but the relationship with him hadn't mended because Romeo hadn't made amends with him. Hadn't taken back the things that he had said. Some of which had been cruel and unfair, but some of which had been true.

They'd had years of difficult conversations, the fallout of the divorce working itself out over the course of years. And never as fully as Romeo might have wished.

"I think we both want to do better. And I'm sorry. I'm sorry that you had such a difficult relationship with him."

He looked at Heather out of the corner of his eye, where she was resting her elbow against the window, looking out at the city.

"He loved me in a way that my own father never did. I never even knew him. My mother marrying him gave me things that were so wonderful, but I never wanted to look at the cost of it. I just ignored that they had an affair. I really did. Because I didn't want either of them to be wrong. It changed my life in such good ways that I didn't want any of it to be wrong. And you had made everything so miserable for me at school."

"I am sorry about that," he said.

Now, with years of perspective, he couldn't fathom why he had done it. Except that he had been angry. At everything. And she had made him feel things that he didn't want to feel, and it had felt like a convenient target for all that rage.

It had felt like an easy thing.

He had really, truly wanted the easy thing.

The bandage for the wound that seemed to be festering there in his chest.

"Thank you," she said. "I lost myself there for a little while too. I got wrapped up in what it felt like to be one of you. To win. So a lot of the things that I did to you when I was in high school, that was all because I was angry, and I wanted to get back at you. Later, though I..."

"You wanted me."

"I did. It confused me. I also realized that it wasn't a new feeling. But again it was confusing because..."

"Because I wasn't nice to you," he said.

"No. You weren't."

"And you really couldn't want anyone but me?"

"No."

"Even that idiot that you almost had sex with at that house party?"

"Even him. I just wanted to not feel like something was wrong with me. Like I was different. Because I was so tired of feeling different. You made me feel so different. It's funny that you were so mad about that party. About me and that other guy, because you pushed me there. You're the one that made me feel like I needed to do something extreme to fix myself. So yes, I am sorry for some of the things, but you are no small part of my insecurity."

He tightened his hand on the steering wheel, looked straight ahead. "I'm sorry. That's inexcusable of me. I have been...a bad person."

"No. You did some bad things, I think. Or I don't

know. You're not altogether bad though, is the thing. You really aren't. Which is part of the annoying thing about you. Part of the reason that I could never fully hate you, and it isn't just because you're gorgeous."

"What good thing have you ever seen me do?"

"You were always there for your father, even though your relationship wasn't easy. And you love your mother. I have always understood that a lot of the reason you didn't like me was because you loved her so much."

"I suppose we do know each other, a little bit."

"A little bit."

He was still grappling with the things that she had said when they pulled the car up outside of the restaurant, and he gave the keys to the valet.

They were ushered into the small building into a private dining room, where it was luxurious and quiet.

"I asked the chef to prepare us a selection of his favorite things."

"Oh, that sounds lovely."

"I know that you and your mother moved to Italy from New York."

"Yes. We did."

"I never asked you what it was like to grow up there."

She rested her chin on the back of her hands, looking at him thoughtfully. "No. You didn't. But then, I never asked you about anything before I met you either. Or really anything that you were experiencing after we met."

"True."

"Well, I went back to New York. Because in many ways it always felt like my home. But also on a slightly pettier note, I wanted to know what it was like to live there when I was part of the other half. We grew up in a studio apartment. It was tiny, and my mom did her best to keep it clean. She worked on the Upper East Side. Sometimes in the summer I would ride the subway with her. And spend most of the day outside on the playgrounds there. Sometimes I would wander around the Met by myself. Or the natural history museum. Air-conditioned. Nice. During the school year I would get myself to school. And usually I would cook dinner so that she would have something when she got home. She didn't ask me to do that. But I wanted to. It was us against the world."

"And then my father put out a ridiculous ad for a housekeeper after he and my mother had a fight."

"What?"

"Did you not know that? It came about because of a fight that they had. My mother was constantly chasing cleaners away by nitpicking their work. And my father said the only way that we would be able to get someone new is by finding them outside the country. And that once he did, my mother was not permitted to engage with the new cleaner. He also said that he would have to pay more than handsomely for them to keep the job. That is how that job posting ended up being the way it was. So generous that of course your mother would never turn it down."

"He fell in love with her at first sight," Heather said, looking down at her hands.

Romeo was about to respond to that when the waiter came in with a charcuterie, an array of meat and cheese. A glass of wine for him, and sparkling water for Heather.

"Did he?" Romeo asked. And he found he wasn't as angry as he used to be.

"Yes. He wanted to give her everything. That was why he offered to send me to the private school. He wanted...he wanted her to notice him the way that he did her. But he wanted to be careful because he was her boss. My mother worked for a lot of rich men. She didn't have relationships with them. And she didn't trust them just because they were rich and men. She knew better than that. It wasn't like it was a pattern with her or anything like that."

"I don't really know what I thought. It feels...salacious on the surface."

"Yes. It does. But it wasn't."

He nodded slowly. "I did see that. In the fullness of time. That what they had was real. It didn't ease anything, though, because it only made me feel all that much more protective of my mother."

"Why wouldn't it? It's a tangle."

"It was never your fault, though."

"No," she said. "It wasn't."

He very nearly laughed.

Their main courses came out after that—perfectly seared steaks and buttered vegetables. And he was gratified to see that Heather was enjoying the food. When she had first come to tell him about the pregnancy she had looked pale and unwell.

Now she seemed much better.

Taking care of her was…satisfying.

He had always felt a strange sort of possessiveness over her. It had been, initially, that she was the woman he hated more than anyone else in all the world.

But now she was his. In a different way.

It made him want to do things differently. Behave differently.

To treat her differently.

"What was it like growing up in your house?"

"I told you. Contentious."

"You said war zone."

He nodded slowly. "They were not a good match. All they did was make each other miserable. My father was rich. My mother was beautiful, and volatile. He didn't know what he was getting into, but they married each other. Based on my math, I assume it's because she was pregnant with me. I was the reason. And therefore, I'm responsible."

"For what?"

"For keeping her happy. At least as happy as she can be, because all of her misery is because of me."

Heather tilted her head to the side. "That isn't true. It's not a fair perspective. You didn't choose to be born, but she chose to have you."

"She couldn't have seen ahead to the consequences."

"Perhaps not. But that doesn't negate her part in it. I could've easily felt that way about my mom. She raised me without any help at all. It was really hard, but she never made me feel like I was a burden. We were family."

"Family, to me, has always meant something different. It has always been something…to do. A challenge."

"I don't want that to be the case for our child."

"Neither do I."

"Did you always want children?"

He shook his head slowly. "To tell you the truth, I hadn't thought about it. In my experience, loving another person is exhausting."

"Your mother?"

"It's a terrible thing to say."

"Maybe. But it's not untrue."

There was nothing more shocking than feeling like maybe the one person who had ever understood this was Heather.

And she had always been there. Yet they had never spoken. Not about this. Not about anything.

They finished their meal, and got back in the car, headed back to the hotel.

As they walked through the lobby, and to the elevator, he looked down at her, and she looked up at him. The expression on her face was soft. Different than any other way she had ever looked at him before. There was understanding there.

Intimacy.

And that had certainly never passed between them before.

The elevator carried them to their floor, and they walked down the hall, to the suite.

He let them both in, and closed the door behind them.

She looked at him, with determination. Her eyes

glittering as she stepped toward him, pressed her hands to his chest and stretched up on her toes to kiss him.

The kiss was soft, tentative at first, but began to increase, deepen.

She tilted her head to the side and parted her lips, sliding her tongue against his.

A shiver went through his body.

They'd had each other hard. They'd had each other mean. This was something else entirely.

There had been very little kissing. Consuming, yes, but no kissing.

He captured the back of her head with his hand, her hair like silk as it slid through his fingers, as he kissed her deeper, longer.

As he wrapped his arm around her and held her hard against his body.

She whimpered. Her fingers curling around the collar of his jacket as she clung to him.

As she deepened the kiss, and it went on and on.

The dress was beautiful. The dress existed so that he could take it off of her.

And this time, he would enjoy her. This time, it wouldn't be fast and hard.

This time, he would take his time.

He lowered the zipper on the dress slowly, watching as it fell away from her body, as it pooled on the floor at her feet.

She was wearing black heels, a black pair of lace panties and a see-through bra. Beautiful.

The way that her red hair contrasted with the dark lace, her pale skin, sent his libido into overdrive.

"You're beautiful," he said, remembering what she had said about giving her compliments. How many things had he said to her that were sharp? Like a cruel sword digging into her skin. He had caused so much pain.

He wanted to erase it now.

"Incredible," he said.

He closed the distance between them, wrapped his arms around her and kissed her neck, her shoulder. "Perfect."

She shivered in his arms, and he unhooked her bra, casting it onto the ground, exposing her glorious flesh, and reveling in the sight.

He kissed her collarbone, down to the plump curve of her breasts, down to her tight, pink nipple, which he drew into his mouth, sucking hard.

"Gorgeous," he said again.

He left praise all over her skin with each kiss, each scrape of his teeth over her delicate skin.

He was not a man who had relationships. He had been preoccupied all of his life with his feelings for her. Such a huge part of himself had always been consumed by the toxicity of what existed between himself and Heather. He had lovers. But there had never been intensity. He had never spent the night in bed with a woman.

He had never lost himself entirely in a kiss, in an orgasm, in a moment.

With her, he was entirely enraptured.

Entirely lost.

"Take me to bed," she whispered against his mouth,

and so he picked her up, and carried her across the living area, back toward that blue canopy bed that had so taken her when they had first arrived.

He thought about everything he had put in their contract. Everything about punishments and domination. But this wasn't the moment for that.

This was the moment to lavish her.

And he had never wanted anything more. Then to make her feel good in that moment.

To undo some of the hurt that he had caused.

He had never done that before. Had never tried to heal anything in himself that was wounded. Had never tried to fix a hurt he'd caused.

Had never tried to take back something that he had said.

He was a man who held grudges. He had done so all of his life.

But he had never tried to repair anything. And each kiss over her skin was an attempt to repair a crack that he had put there.

"Now I want you naked," she said.

She scooted up the bed, resting her elbows against the pillows there. She looked at him, direct and strong. He moved away from her, and began to loosen his tie, unbuttoned his shirt.

"Completely naked. No more of this half-dressed nonsense."

He shrugged off his jacket, unbuttoned his shirt, cast it down to the floor.

And she looked at him, her eyes hungry as he removed every last article of clothing.

"Yes," she said, rising up onto her knees and moving toward the end of the bed. "You are the most beautiful man I've ever seen. I've never wanted another one. In spite of my best efforts."

"You don't need another one," he said.

"Maybe not."

She smiled, just slightly, and he wanted to taste it. So he did.

He got onto the bed, and she moved around him, lightly pushing on his chest and laying him on his back. She hovered over him, her red hair shrouding them both as she leaned in and pressed kisses to his chest.

Down farther. And farther still.

She wrapped her hand around his arousal, and squeezed hard, then licked him from base to tip with the flat of her tongue. He let his head fall back, his breath hissing through his teeth.

"Do you like that?" she asked.

"Yes."

"Do you want more?"

"Yes," he said.

She teased him. Brushed his skin with her hair, nipped at the head of his cock, sucked him in deep and didn't hold him long enough.

She pushed him all the way to the edge, again and again.

He was shaking, sweating. It would've been easy to believe that he was the virgin, and not so recently her.

She bit his hipbone, and he groaned, overcome by his desire for her.

By his need for more.

She moved over him, straddling him, her slick heat glorious against his hardness, and she moved her hips, taking him in an inch, before letting him slip out, denying them both what they so desperately wanted. She did it over and over again, the sensation maddening. Driving him to his limit.

Pushing him to the edge.

"Beg," she said.

"Please," he said.

"My name," she said. "I know you've been with other women. How many?"

"I don't know."

"How many times did you think of me?"

He laughed, dark and humorless. There was nothing funny about any of this.

"Every time," he said.

"Then it is a privilege for you to be able to have me. Isn't it?"

"Yes," he ground out, his hands on her hips.

"Beg me," she said.

"Please, Heather," he said.

She rocked her hips back, and slid onto him, taking him in slowly, letting her head fall back on a sigh when he was buried all the way inside of her.

And then, he could not wait any longer.

He reversed their positions, driving into her, desperate, starving. He kissed her. Deep and hard while he was buried inside of her. She moved her hands up over her head, and he gathered them in his palm, holding her wrists together as he continued to take her.

He was lost. In this, in her. He had never experienced anything like this before. Anything like her.

And as he growled out his satisfaction, she cried out her own, clenching tightly around him and sending him into another time and space.

And tomorrow he would be with her, sitting across from his mother.

He let out a hard breath that was nearly a laugh as he collapsed, taking hold of her face and kissing her, the endorphin release so strong it took him by surprise.

"What?" she asked, looking up at him.

"Nothing. It is only that you will be the only woman I've ever slept with to meet my mother."

"And that's funny?"

"It's only… Our relationship makes it mildly amusing, I suppose."

"I would prefer not to think about your other lovers," she said, burrowing into the covers.

"But if we stick to our agreement it's possible that both of us will have them," he said.

"Possible," she returned.

Jealousy and possessiveness gripped him.

He did not like the idea, of course. But the idea of binding them both to a traditional marriage when they had never had any sort of relationship that wasn't antagonistic before the last week or so seemed foolish at best.

Hell, it had barely been a week of them getting along.

And ninety percent of it had been fucking. They did quite well when it came to that.

"I feel that I have to warn you about my mother," he said. "She is sometimes the most delightful and engaging person you've ever met. And other times…"

"I think you're forgetting that I *have* met your mother."

"No, I'm not. But whatever aspects of her erratic nature you experienced back then, it is worse now."

"I'm an editor," she said. "Do you have any idea the number of erratic personalities that I work with at a given time? Writers are not the most mentally stable people."

He chuckled. "Are they not?"

"No. Typically, they are emotional, often missing deadlines, and then you have to try to manage their stress all while dealing with yours, and trying to make them feel like they're geniuses, while gently suggesting they fix the dreck that you received from them. It's a tightrope. I'm good at walking it. You know, initially I was going into publicity, and I thought that I would use it in the hospitality business. But what I've discovered is that part of being an editor is engaging in customer service."

"I hadn't thought of that."

"Of course not. I didn't get into the job for that. I thought it would be reading, and helping shape stories, and I am. I love it. But I also have to figure out which stories are going to make money, and present that to a team, make the case for it. I have to attend more meetings during the week than I would like, though I've been let off the hook from a few of them because of the time difference. A lot of the reading I do on my own time."

"I'm surprised, in many ways, that you didn't pursue work under the Accardi banner."

"Of course you are. Because you always thought that was what I wanted. I'm not going to say that I didn't get a lot out of suddenly becoming rich overnight. Of course I did. But it wasn't all quite the way that you thought."

"I see that now."

"Why did you end up getting into that business when you were so angry at your father?"

"I wanted to prove to him that given the same arena I could do better than he did. But I was valuable, perhaps."

"He was proud of you."

He didn't know what to say to that, so he didn't say anything. He had never talked about these things with anyone else. But no one had ever asked him these sorts of questions.

She was interesting. The way she spoke about her work. The way she wanted to know about his.

He had branded her as something frivolous. Pointless. Because it had been convenient for him to do so, and yet on some level he must've known there was more to her. More to her than he had wanted to see. Than he had wanted to acknowledge. But it felt so much simpler to cast everyone in black and white, as he did his level best to keep his mother from imploding. It was easier to see things the way that she did. The appropriate people as villains.

And certainly not…

He certainly couldn't afford to be anyone else's savior.

That night that he had stopped Heather's sexual encounter with that man, he had been filled with such a deep, profound sense of rage and possessiveness. It had been nearly overwhelming, and he had no more room in him for that. Anger was easy. Wanting to protect less so.

It had a cost. Such an intense cost.

"Don't worry about your mother," she said, kissing him on the shoulder. The simple affectionate gesture nearly took his breath away.

"Sadly, Heather," he said, lying on his back and staring at the ceiling. "I have been doing nothing but worrying about her for the last twenty years. I'm not going to stop just because you told me to."

"But what if you did?" she whispered.

And without giving it too much thought, he fell asleep with a woman beside him.

CHAPTER TEN

SHE WOULD BE lying if she said she wasn't nervous about meeting with Romeo's mom. She was obviously very important to him, and a huge part of their issues came from the fact that the divorce had hurt her so much. And Heather had been lumped up into the grouping of very bad things that had caused trauma.

She figured it was in her best interest to dress demurely so as not to draw attention to herself or bring up any feelings about her being some kind of seductress who had trapped Romeo into this. "I have trapped you into marriage, though," she said cheerfully as they got into his car and began to drive toward his mother's home.

"Have you?"

"Yes. The ultimatum that I issued you was quite firm."

"I truly hate to be the one to tell you this, but you effectively couldn't trap me if you wanted to. You might have inherited a sizable fortune from my father, which we split, but don't forget I was already in possession of my own."

That made her bristle. "What are you saying?"

"You don't have as much power over me as you think."

She gazed at the Austrian countryside, which was beautiful, particularly in comparison to how annoyed she felt just at the moment.

"But you agreed."

"Yes. Because I think it's the best thing. I don't think that our child should experience the difficulties that either of us did. And I think that it's best, for many reasons, for the two of us to be married. But if I had decided not to marry you, I would never have surrendered full custody just because you said that was my only option."

"That is really annoying."

"Why? Why does it matter, when you got your way?"

"It matters because..." Well, now she felt manipulated.

"You wanted to think that you got something on your own?"

"Maybe. Or like maybe I was compelling."

"You are compelling, Heather Gray. If you weren't, I wouldn't have gotten you pregnant in the first place."

That placated her slightly. But only slightly. At least she had some pull, she supposed.

His mother's house was beautiful. Palatial and situated on top of a mountain that overlooked the city.

"Beautiful," she said.

"It is," he replied. "You would think that she might find some peace here."

"She doesn't?"

"Peace is not really in my mother's wheelhouse."

Her stomach twisted with nerves, or maybe it was morning sickness. It was really hard to tell. She had been feeling better in general, but sometimes nausea hit her, and not necessarily always early in the day.

They were ushered in by one of his mother's employees, and through the entryway, into the dining room. It was set up beautifully for high tea, with tiered trays of desserts and delicate china all around.

"This is beautiful."

Heather said that just before his mother swept into the room, and the look of delight on her face at hearing it instantly alleviated some of Heather's worries.

"I'm glad that you think so," she said.

Carla Accardi was one of the most beautiful women in the world. This was a truth universally accepted by many fashion magazines, and age had not dimmed her beauty. Her dark hair was just as it had been the last time Heather had seen her. Long and falling in waves around her shoulders, not a single strand of silver to be seen, though that was probably the work of color artists.

She still had the slim frame required of a runway model back in the '90s, and as Heather remembered, looked elegant just standing there. She was wearing a floral robe in a highly saturated silk. It could have been a dress, it could've been only a robe, but she made it look like high-fashion either way.

"Lisa's daughter," she said, her dark eyes fixed like lasers on Heather.

"Yes."

"Your mother is dead now."

"Yes," Heather said.

There was no real compassion in the other woman's voice. But no venom either. It was an observation. And even though it felt unkind, Heather wasn't going to react to it. She had too much practice being bullied.

"Let's all have a seat," Carla said, smiling brightly.

Heather returns the smile. "Yes. Let's."

"You're pregnant," Carla said, in that same matter-of-fact tone. No indication as to whether or not she was pleased by the news.

"Yes. And Romeo and I are getting married. I know he told you already."

"I do hope that you have a prenuptial agreement."

"Yes," Romeo said. "We do. Of course. To protect the both of us."

"You obviously need more protection than she does," Carla said.

"Financially," Heather said, shrugging. "That is inarguably true."

Both Romeo and Carla looked at her.

"Well," she said. "It is. I'm not offended by that."

"Is he only marrying you because you're pregnant?" she asked.

The question was cutting. But again, nothing that had never been leveled at Heather before. By Romeo himself, in fact.

"Yes. We both think it would be better to avoid the messy situation that we found ourselves in growing up."

"I'm familiar with the mess," Carla said.

"I know," Heather responded. "I wasn't casting any blame. It must've hurt you very much, what happened between my mother and your husband. I know that it's ancient history now, and both of them are gone. But it doesn't change the fact that it's a painful history."

Heather wasn't being disingenuous. She might believe that Giuseppe and her mother were the love story, but it didn't mean there was no cost to it. As a kid, she had filtered that out. Because it had been inconvenient to think about it or dwell on it. Because it didn't feel beneficial. But as an adult, she could look at it with a little bit more complexity. Now that she was not looking at Romeo as an enemy, now that she was actually giving some space to how his relationship with his father had been damaged, and it was entirely on him, she was just…seeing it differently.

"I was very hurt by it," Carla said. "Thank you."

"I promise that I don't want to hurt your son in any way. And we're going to be the best parents possible for your grandchild. You're their only grandparent. The only one they have left. The only one they'll ever know. That's an incredibly special position."

It wasn't about placating her, or managing her, though she was well aware she was doing that, but it really was about the relationship. Romeo couldn't fix the relationship with his father. He was gone. Their child wouldn't have another grandparent.

"That is a very…kind thing to say," Carla said.

"It's true," Heather said.

"We're building a family. I think it can be a good thing."

"I would like to wear green to your wedding," Carla said.

"Of course you can," Heather replied.

"I prefer a Kelly green."

"You can wear whatever shade you want. And I will choose whatever shade I like for everything else." On that she was firm. His mother would not be taking over every aspect of the wedding.

Of course, maybe it didn't matter if the wedding was… Was it a sham wedding? They were getting married for the baby? They weren't in love—they…

They certainly had a sexual relationship. Right now. But all of their paperwork had all those contingencies, and if they had sex while they were married, the stakes of it all went up.

But it was the only marriage she would have.

She had never really dreamed of marriage, or having children. Because the way that Romeo had obsessed her, wrapped himself around her desires and her fantasies at such a young age, had kept her from doing so.

And now she was marrying him. Consigning herself to life with him while they raised their child—it was what they had both agreed on. But she couldn't see life after Romeo, because she had never been able to see life after Romeo. And in the one moment when she had thought she might have a life after him, she had cut her own fantasy short by finally snapping the thread that had stretched between them for all this time.

She'd crossed a line with him and couldn't go back. So as far as she was concerned, the marriage was real.

The marriage was *real*.

What she didn't know was how to ensure it was still about their child.

Because right now that was a distant hope, and Romeo was here now. She wanted him, she craved him, but she also knew they'd only been getting along for about forty-eight hours.

That thought echoed inside of her as she tried to finish her tea. But that left so many unanswered questions. If it was real, then what were her feelings toward him? And what was she going to do when they walked down the aisle with all that paperwork between them?

Was there a world where they could try to make something real out of all of this?

When they left, he walked around to her side of the car and pulled the door open. He looked at her for a long moment. "You did amazingly well."

She got into the car, and he shut the door, and she released a shuddering breath on a realization.

She had never really hated him at all.

The way that she handled his mother had been skillful on a level he had never seen before. Moreover, she had made it seem easy. He had expected some kind of blowup, but that hadn't occurred. Instead, Heather had seemed to know exactly what to say and what to do. And though his mother was…happy with the arrangement, at least for now, he knew better than anyone how quickly his mother's moods could change. But he was pleased to be in the middle of a good one now.

Everything was working out well right now. But he had never been more aware of exactly what was at stake. The ecosystem was fragile. Between him and Heather, everyone and his mother. The environment that they were bringing their child into had the potential to be volatile. He had never experienced family any other way.

The idea of Heather being with someone else filled him with a rage that he couldn't quantify, but that in and of itself told him that he had to change the way that he was thinking about her.

The way that he was thinking about their relationship.

They had been enemies. They had now been lovers. Perhaps there was some world where they could be friends. That might be the only way to guarantee that their child experienced some form of stability.

The way that she had dealt with Carla...

He had never seen anything like it.

He wanted to *always* have that.

Passion was what his parents'd had. For a time. Then it had become hatred. He'd experienced hatred with Heather, and he felt like it was a tightrope walk. Easy, so easy for them to end up right back there, and what would that mean for their child?

He intended to do what the adults in his life had never quite managed.

To put that child first.

When they left Vienna, they went back to the estate, and he manufactured business that needed to be done in London—even though he could've done it anywhere. While he was away he sent Heather a text.

Perhaps you could spend some time back in New York. It would probably be good for you to check in with your job. Attend some of those meetings you like so much.

What made you change your mind on that?

Our wedding is set for a month from now. I trust you.

There. He was being kind. Shortly she would interpret his actions as kindness. This was the problem. He didn't want to tell her that he thought they shouldn't be lovers and have her afraid that it was because of something she had done wrong. It was, in fact, because of something that she had done exceptionally well. It was because he had seen a potential that he now longed to make reality.

They'd never had a friendship. And the feelings that fueled the desire between them were inarguably founded on toxicity.

That wasn't good for anyone.

She did send him messages about the wedding, and he enjoyed her including him in the process. She did go to New York, and she kept him up-to-date on the various meetings that she had to attend, and the absolute author meltdown she had wrangled.

She called the lead publicist thirteen times. Like we can't see who's calling. She called everyone. And then whenever Caroline's assistant would answer, she would hang up.

What was she mad about?

She didn't get as many trade reviews as she thinks she should. She's mad at the whole publicity department.

There was a pause in their texting. Then she sent another:

What are you working on?

Her question surprised him. Developing a new route on the cruise line, and negotiating port contracts. Cruise traffic is in such a state right now that you have to have rights to get your passengers dropped off right at the fork. I'm trying to make sure that our line has the most optimum placement.

Well, it's not author tantrums.

No. It isn't.

What he didn't expect was for her to arrive in London without announcement at the town house where she had her ill-fated graduation party all those years ago.

But there she was, glowing in the middle of the entryway when he got home, her body curvier than when she had left nearly a month ago, her smile unlike anything he had ever seen before. Had Heather ever smiled at him like this? No. Of course she hadn't. Because there had been nothing but bad blood between them for all that time. And now she was smiling at him. Like he was something wonderful.

It felt weighted. Like there was an expectation behind it. Because how could there be anything else? That meant that he had to keep them here. In this place, where it was only a smile. Where he could not fail her.

"I didn't expect you," he said.

She blinked, and then moved toward him. He moved slightly, and the kiss that had been intended for his mouth landed on his cheek. There was something all the more damning about that. All the more intense. He gritted his teeth and took a step back. "I need to speak with you, and I confess that I was putting it off."

"Oh?"

She looked afraid. Ready for battle, then, and why would she? It had always been a battle between them. There'd been so little time where they had been cordial. Where they had been anything like friends.

"Don't look at me like that. Like I'm going to bite you. I'm not."

"You look like it," she said. "And not in a fun way."

He nodded once. "Come and sit down."

"Should I remind you that the invitations to the wedding have already been sent out?"

"I don't need to be reminded of that. I'm not backing out of this. But I have been thinking about the future. About what our home will look like, will feel like for our child. What you said to my mother has been weighing on me heavily."

"What?"

"She is the last remaining grandparent. And whether we would have chosen it or not, the three of us are now family. We must make a family for our child. I love my mother very much. But she is not an easy woman.

She never has been. I assume she will be difficult in the future as well. Even if she doesn't mean to be. I will always have to shoulder the responsibility of caring for her. But the way that you spoke with her, the way that you were with her, it made me… It made me realize what I truly want for our child."

"What?"

"Peace. For the adults in his or her life to put them first. As no one ever did with us. I know that you had a better experience with your father and mother in the household, but when your father left your mother, he didn't think of you. He didn't put you first. Your mother did, though. And you have greatly benefited from that. My father and my mother put their own feelings first. Always. And I have always borne the brunt of that. You and I are looking at eighteen years of attempting to create harmony, and we've had a couple of months where we have done well with each other. And you were away for a substantial portion of it."

"Please get to the point. You're an infamous, ruthless businessman, and you're talking around me like a car salesman. We both know that's not you."

"I don't want to hurt you. I don't want you to think it's anything you've done wrong. I have been cruel to you, I accept responsibility for that. This is not cruelty. But you and I need to set aside our attraction."

"What?"

"I have only ever seen passion go badly."

"My mother and your father loved each other very much. Until the end."

"They had a love story—that much is certain. But

I believe that it was founded very much on my father's desire to rescue her. And in many ways, I feel that your mother wanted to rescue him. They did. But my parents… They married because of me. Because she was pregnant. They married because their passion drove them together. And it kept driving them. It was toxic. So were they."

"If it was so terrible then why were you mad when they got divorced?"

"Because it doesn't end—that's what I'm trying to tell you. It doesn't burn itself out. My mother never could let go of it. And I know there are other reasons for that. I know that it has to do with her depressive episodes, but it doesn't change the reality. Leaving my father, the dissolution of the marriage, it didn't fix anything. Not between the two of them, and not between us. I had to be my mother's savior, and that made me my father's adversary, and he couldn't pull himself out of that either because his feelings for her were so twisted up at that point. We can never be that for our child."

He could see the hurt in her eyes, the confusion. But she wouldn't always be hurt or confused. She wouldn't be.

"This is a trick. Of our imaginations, of our hormones. I want for us to de-escalate the feelings. This has been good, this last month. We've communicated. And it feels like a foundation. Fucking on tables is not the foundation for a happy life for a child. You and I could follow that until it burns us both out, but to what end? That isn't why we are getting married, and maybe if you hadn't gotten pregnant we could've explored that. But you did. And we must be in this together."

She took a breath, and there was a single break at the center of it. But it never became a sob. Her eyes remained dry. "You're right. Of course you are. Because we are asking each other to do something impossible. To know, without a shadow of a doubt, that this relationship that we're trying to build is going to last until our child is an adult. Everyone intends for that to be the case. Surely that was why your parents got married. And then they couldn't do it. They couldn't manage it."

"To be fair to them, I suppose they did make it into my adulthood."

"Close. But you still bore the weight of the consequences. And you lived in a war zone, as you said. And when we are at our worst…"

"When we are at our worst it's very bad."

"Yes. I agree with that."

It was so much harder now that she was here. Because he wanted her. Wanted to touch her. Wanted to hold her. Wanted to draw her against his body and feel her heart beating beneath his hand. To move his hands over her curves and make her his. Definitively.

But they would marry. And they would be tied together. She would be his. Just not in that way.

"I'm probably going to go back to the estate," she said. "I'm glad that I was able to stop and see you."

"You might as well spend the night here."

"It's only a two-hour flight to Italy. I'll just head there."

"You came here for me," he said, his voice rougher than intended.

She wanted him.

God knew he wanted her.

He was trying. Trying to make the right choice, and where Heather was concerned he had a low success rate with that. He wanted her to want him, even as he wanted some distance and sanity where she was concerned.

A small smile curved the corner of her lips. "No. Of course not. I just came here to talk about our friendship. I'm glad that I did. I'm glad that we are on the same page."

He knew that she was lying. But of course he was going to allow her to have the lie.

"I'll see you in Vienna. For the wedding."

"I have a dress."

"Good. I'm glad to hear it."

Need flooded his veins. She looked away from him, and her red hair slid over her shoulder, catching the lamplight, gold playing over the top of the fiery strands. He wanted to touch them. Wanted to touch her. He wouldn't let himself.

He had never been one for exercising discipline when it came to Heather. But he did it in so many other areas of his life. He hadn't become as successful as he was without it. He worked day and night, he catered to his mother, he had brief, satisfying relationships with women who knew that he was never going to get emotionally invested. Because he didn't have any more to give. He was going to have to find more for his child.

There could never be anything else. He needed something that he could draw more from, not something that would take from him. And truthfully, the relationship with Heather filled the well inside of him in ways that nothing else had.

He needed her. Needed her by his side more than he needed her underneath. He was simply going to have to remember that.

"After the wedding we could start talking about the nursery. Find out whether the baby is a boy or a girl. That will be nice."

"It will be."

She gave him a smile before she walked out of the room, out of the town house, and he paced over to the bar, grabbing a bottle of Scotch and pouring himself a measure of it. Then he walked up to the wall and smashed his elbow right through the Sheetrock. The pain was searing, and he looked at the white shirt he was wearing and saw that it was red with blood.

He let it run.

There was pain now. So that there could be peace later.

He was standing solid in that.

She had been mildly devastated by the conversation they'd had at the London house. She hadn't expected it. Yes, she had found it disquieting that he had suggested she leave, but she hadn't put a lot of extra thought into it. She had hoped that it was actually a good-faith gesture, which was how he had presented it. That he trusted her, so she could go and be in New York for a while if it suited her.

She hadn't expected for him to cut her off entirely. For their sexual relationship to end just like that.

Logically though, she had been thinking that they would end it at least for a while when they got married, until they got their footing and then...

She had known that they would never be able to resist each other, so obviously they would end up back in bed and then maybe he... Maybe he would begin to feel the same way that she did.

Her chest was sore. But she looked amazing. She had bought the most beautiful wedding dress that she had ever seen. A sweetheart neckline with crystals all over. It was short underneath, with a sheer overlay, glimmering with all of those glass beads. Her legs were visible when the light hit it just right.

And she had the most risqué bustier that she could find beneath it, along with a pair of panties that might as well not even be there for all that they were as substantial as cobwebs.

But that felt like where they were heading. It had been her fantasy, of a wedding night, of the way that things could be between them, and he had decisively ended it. She couldn't even argue with what he had said.

It was impossible to argue with. They were getting married because she was pregnant. Not because they wanted each other.

She stood there, looking at her reflection in the mirror for a long moment.

It had been four days since she had last seen him, and now it was the wedding day.

And she felt…sad.

Just a little bit sad.

But also determined that this was the right thing. Them getting married was the best thing.

"You look beautiful," Catherine said.

She turned to face her closest friend, and did her best to smile. Catherine didn't know all the details of everything that was happening with her and Romeo, and she was pretty skeptical of the fact that he had suddenly become a decent human being. In fact, she had called Heather sex addled on more than one occasion.

But now that she was here, at the wedding, she seemed to be a lot more accepting.

Or maybe she had just accepted that Heather was going to do what she had decided, and wasn't going to be deterred from it.

"Thank you for making me your maid of honor."

"You're my best friend," Heather said. "I thought about having a whole big bridal party, but all of those people… I don't really know them anymore. Mind you, we have a huge contingent from our years at Fairfield here. Because the absolute spectacle of the two of us getting married was too much to resist."

"I would say. I never got to see the two of you spark off of each other. You were obsessed with him."

She looked back at her own reflection. The largeness of her eyes, the color in her cheeks. "I'm still obsessed with him."

"That's good, since you're marrying him."

"I guess. I guess it's good. But we have to raise a child and not implode. We don't have a lot of practice with not imploding. We're…a whole storm."

"I'm glad that the sex is good," Catherine said, dryly.

Heather laughed. "That's not the only thing I meant."

"I know. But clearly the sex is good."

"It's all-consuming. Which concerns me."

She was hedging around the truth.

"He's gorgeous. So, I get it. Though I've had sex with some pretty gorgeous men who turned out to be disappointing."

"Nothing about Romeo is disappointing."

"I think you might just love him."

She stopped, and of course Catherine was going to say that, because she didn't know about the contract, about the agreement. She didn't know about the connective tissue of all the moments they'd spent together since then. That he had never professed to have any sort of emotional connection with her. Nothing other than a desire for friendship, which was why he was determined not to touch her.

"You think I love him?"

"You're marrying him. In a gorgeous white dress. You look like you're glowing. You're having his baby. You're obsessed with his body. What part of that doesn't sound like love to you?"

"Isn't love supposed to be soft and wonderful?"

"No," Catherine sighed. "Listen, I'm not an expert. I've had some relationships that have burned themselves out quickly, and I've had some that have lasted longer. I haven't found the love of my life. I certainly never wanted the same man for nearly fifteen years, and nothing, not the passage of time or the way that he treated me, or the way that I treated him, could change the way that I felt. So I mean, there's that. Mainly though, I think love is a lot like the rest of life. It changes with us. Moves with us. I think it can be comfortable. Something lived in and lovely. But sometimes it has teeth. Sometimes you leave bite marks all over it because you're trying so hard to hold on. I don't think love is any one thing. It's too big for that."

Her words echoed through Heather. And it was difficult for her to deny them.

It had been him. From the beginning.

When he had stood there by the pool looking at her over the top of his sunglasses like she was nothing, and he had suddenly become everything.

She had watched him go from a beautiful boy to a beautiful man. She had tried to want something else, and she had never quite managed it.

"I spent so many years not even liking him."

"Is it that simple? Did you not like him? Or were you just desperate for him, and it felt like dislike? Desperate for his attention while he was seducing other women, and in general being mean to you."

"I…"

Desperate for his attention. That resonated. It echoed inside of her. Yes, she had been desperate for his attention. Desperate for him to see her. She had tried to shape herself into the kind of girl that would interest him, that would catch his focus, and when all she could get was his disdain, she had learned to feed off of that.

"We're worse than I thought. Because you're right. I never hated him. At all. I wanted him desperately in whatever form that took. And I was willing to have it be hard. Mean."

Catherine reached out and squeezed Heather's arm. "You're just a girl."

"What does that mean?"

"Who among us hasn't been absolutely wretched for a gorgeous man? A man who captures us no matter how bad of an idea it is. It is definitive proof that you can't choose your sexuality. Because God knows I would've been done with men ages ago."

She was about to protest again. There was no way they could love each other because there was so much…anger there.

But there hadn't been. Not recently. He was the first person that she texted in the morning, and the last before she went to bed. He had been her first thought all day, every day for the last fifteen years.

She wished she could deny that it was love.

She wished she could write it off as obsession. As something temporary or shallow, but nothing with teeth that penetrated this deeply could ever be shallow.

Nothing that had lasted this long.

She couldn't think about other men. She couldn't want them. She cared what he thought about her, so much so that she'd been performing at him in a variety of ways for years. She'd been sick over him, so much so she'd hoped to never see him again and then had destroyed that plan by sleeping with him, getting pregnant with his baby.

And now she knew they could actually like each other too.

That she could enjoy his company instead of only feeling like her skin was too tight when she was near him.

"I love him," she whispered.

"Yes, you do," Catherine said. "It really is a good thing that you're marrying him."

"I suppose."

But he had said that they needed to continue to pursue the friendship part of things. But there would never be another man for her. Not ever. And she wasn't prepared to let him go off and be with other women. She wasn't… She wasn't only doing this for their child. She was doing this for her too. Because she wanted him. She didn't just want to be a vessel for this life inside of her. She didn't just want to be a mother. She wanted to be a whole woman. Who had love. It was one thing she had never begrudged her mother, not just because it had improved their circumstances, but because Heather had always known that her mother deserved that kind of happiness.

Romeo simply hadn't been raised by a woman who had allowed him that feeling. His mother had often been miserable, and she had made her son feel miserable when she did.

His emotional state was so tied to her that of course he saw it more simply.

If they were happy, and at peace, their child would be.

But life was too dynamic for that.

And they were already too complicated. But that wasn't something to run from.

"You don't look happy."

"I am," Heather said.

Because for the first time, everything made sense. For the first time, she made sense. For the first time, all of this felt right.

She wasn't going to let him run away from this.

She had to believe that she still had power. To change his mind. To make things shift.

Catherine handed Heather her bright pink bouquet, and she took hold of it and gave herself one last, purposeful look in the mirror before the two of them walked down to the chapel.

It was absolutely packed full of people, because who could resist coming to gawk at this?

Not many that had been invited, it turned out.

The whole thing looked like an elegant wonderland, with twisting branches woven together with fairy lights wound around them. Making an arbor for her to walk beneath as she made her way up the aisle. And there he was. Stern and stoic in his black suit, his black hair ruthlessly styled off of his forehead.

Romeo. Her stepbrother. The father of her baby. Her husband.

Hers. Inevitably. There was no escaping him, and she didn't even want to.

She wanted him. She wanted this. Forever. He took

her hand, and looked at her. His gaze drifted down to her cleavage, and back up. And just like when they had been teenagers, she knew.

He had made a mistake.

He wanted her.

When they spoke their vows, her heart began to beat harder. Faster. She meant every word. This was no performance.

Standing there in front of all these people, in front of Catherine in her pink bridesmaid dress, and Carla in her kelly-green mother-of-the-bride gown. This was real for her. The only wedding she would ever have.

"You may now kiss the bride."

They hadn't discussed this beforehand. But there was no need to discuss it. She knew what she wanted.

She wrapped her arms around his neck and kissed him. Deep and long. With all the desire that she had inside her body. He captured the back of her head, his tongue sweeping over hers, clearly overcome just as she was. He wasn't going to stop this now. He wasn't going to stop.

No. He kissed her deep and long, the desire that was building inside of her aching and desperate, even in front of all these people.

This was what everyone had come to see, so they might as well see it. This need that existed between the two of them.

It was real.

And it was strong. No matter what he said.

He pulled away from her, his breathing hard, the

color in his cheekbones dark red, suggesting pent-up desire.

Oh yes. He did want her.

She was going to get her wedding night. And what she had that. He wouldn't be able to have anyone else, not without consequences.

She loved him. That wasn't making her feelings soft.

She could try to be his friend. But she wanted to be his lover. His wife. His woman.

She wasn't going to give the man peace.

He was going to have to work for it.

On that she was determined.

CHAPTER ELEVEN

HE HAD SEEN the challenge in her eyes. But worse was the moment that he had first seen her coming up the aisle in her wedding dress.

Like a dream. All white satin and glimmering jewels.

The shape of her body tempting him. Calling to him.

He had never seen such a beautiful woman.

Never.

It had been that way from the beginning.

Yes, she had been young when she first arrived. And his feelings hadn't been like that. But once she had begun to develop into a woman, he had been... captivated.

When she had come toward him in that dress, he had been reminded of the day by the pool when they had both been in high school. When he had been unable to keep his eyes off of the glory of her curves. When he had been unable to do anything but stare at how beautiful she was. So beautiful.

But it wasn't only that; it was the feeling of possessiveness. She was his. His wife.

And the challenge as she leaned in to kiss him...

Now they were back in that hotel in Vienna, where they had stayed last time, and it was heavy with memories. Memories of the last time they had stayed here, and what they had done in the beds. On the floor. Against the wall.

They had done it. It should be over. He didn't want this. He didn't want this sharp, awful feeling riding him all the time. He wanted what they'd had when she was a continent away. But they couldn't be separated by a continent, because they had to raise a child together.

He needed a Scotch.

But his suit was choking him.

He went into his bedroom, and it would be his bedroom—they had discussed this ahead of time, because they had an agreement—and closed the door behind him. Then he went to the sideboard where there was a decanter of Scotch, and stood there staring at it as he undid the cuffs on his shirt, undid his tie. He unbuttoned his shirt and slid it off along with his jacket, letting them fall to the floor. And then he took the top off the decanter of Scotch, very aware that if this was how he was going to cope with his feelings for her, he was going to be drinking a lot more than he should.

And how would that make him an exemplary father?

He had no idea. He didn't have a plan. This was entirely fucked.

He was aware of that. He also had no answer to it.

He lifted up his glass, and brought it to his lips, just as he heard the sound of the door opening behind him. He froze. He didn't turn around.

He heard her footsteps, and then she was just behind him. She reached around and took hold of the glass, setting it in front of him on the sideboard before wrapping her arms around his midsection. Her palms flat against his stomach. Then she began to let her fingers drift, one moving up over his nipple, the other moving down to cup his raging hard-on.

"Heather," he said, his voice a warning.

"I know," she said. "If we do this, then this is how it is. If we do this, then we have to contend with all of it, don't we?" While she spoke she was stroking him, and it felt so good he couldn't bring himself to stop her.

He didn't want to stop her.

He was a fool.

"We could be friends, Romeo. We can have peace, but there's always going to be this. Always. And I've decided that I can't accept that. I cannot let you inside of another woman." She wrapped her fingers around his cock through the fabric of his pants. And squeezed. "It's mine," she said. "You are mine."

He turned around on a growl, gripping her face, holding it steady in his palm. "Is this what you want? Because let me warn you. If this is how you want to play it, it isn't going to be soft or nice. If this belongs to you," he said, putting her palm flat against him again, "you belong to me. All of you." He traced the line of her jaw, down the side of her neck, and palmed her breast. Squeezing. "Mine." Then he moved his hand between her legs, stroking her through the thin fabric of her gown, feeling her heat, feeling that she was damp. "And this is mine."

"Yes," she said, her throat tight. "That's the agreement that we have. And that's what I want. That's what I want."

"You're asking for everything we agreed to?"

"Everything," she said.

She took a step away from him, her hand behind her back as she unzipped her dress and let it fall to the floor in a shimmering puddle at her feet. He growled when he saw what she had on beneath. A white lace undergarment that held her breasts up on display, showed the shadow of her nipples beneath the lace. A pair of panties so small they covered nothing. Rather they only served as a tease.

"I bought this for you in New York. Before you told me that you wanted to be friends. At the very least, I thought you should have the chance to see it."

"You're playing with fire."

"I know. I have been. For all these years, and that became so very clear to me today. I want everything. I want you."

"Then you get everything."

His hands were shaking. "But don't think you won't pay a price for it. You have been begging me to be punished."

Arousal clouded her eyes. "I have been."

"Because you've been a brat from the moment I met you. And you know what happens to brats."

"They get what they deserve. You were going to let me off far too easily."

Those words ignited something in his veins.

With one hand he undid his belt and pulled it

through the loops. Then he moved to her, wrapping his belt around her wrists and putting the end of it through the buckle, pulling tight, binding her, as he had promised her he would do in their contract. And what she had explicitly added back in.

"My bratty stepsister's finally ready for the punishment she deserves?"

"Yes," she said.

He grabbed the end of the belt and pulled her toward the bed, where he sat on the edge and laid her across his knee. He looked at the back of the bustier she was wearing, an intricate series of hooks and eyes keeping her body wrapped in all that lace. Nearly all of her gorgeous ass was exposed by her thong, and it made his mouth water. He squeezed her cheek, and then slapped it hard. She squeaked, and jumped.

"If you say stop, I'll stop."

"You don't think I can handle you?"

"I know you can, but I also know that your stubbornness gets you into trouble," he said, smacking her on her ass again.

"I want trouble."

And he wanted to do this for her, because she wanted it. And he relished that. That she trusted him like this. That she was happy to have her hands bound, happy to surrender not just her pleasure, but the perfect amount of pain. It made him feel powerful. But at the same time it made him feel like begging.

To have her like this always.

He left her skin gloriously red, and she was whimpering on his lap, trying to ride his thigh to get some satisfaction. He pushed his fingers through her folds and found her slick and wet. "You enjoyed that."

"So did you," she said, her hand moving to his cock.

"You are such a brat."

"And you want me," she said.

He lifted her from his lap, and pushed her up to the edge of the bed, propped up on her knees, as he tugged her panties down to her mid-thigh. He looked at her, glistening and glorious, and leaned in, thrusting his tongue deep inside of her, tasting her desire.

She came instantly, trembling and shivering, and crying out his name.

His. All his.

Oh God, he might be sending them both to hell right now. But she was his. In a way that no one had ever been. In a way that nothing had ever been.

This was triumph like he had never known. And he would give her whatever she wanted in order to keep it. He stripped himself naked, and he pulled her into a sitting position so he could undo all the hooks and eyes on that bustier, letting it fall away, letting him see those gorgeous curves. Pale and pink, more generous now than they ever had been.

The evidence of her pregnancy aroused him much more than he would've ever imagined. The evidence that he had claimed her. That she was his.

He freed her hands. Set her loose.

"Lay down," she said.

It was his turn to obey. Because he had agreed to it. He did not take orders from women. Not generally.

But there was enough power between them to exchange it. At least for now.

He lay on his back, and she moved over the top of him, biting down on his neck. "You will always belong to me."

He gripped her hair, pulling her down to him and kissing her deep, reveling in the feeling of her nipples brushing against his chest.

Then he released her, and let her kiss her way down his body. She teased him. Bringing him to the edge with her mouth again then again.

Taking him to the edge of himself. Places he had never been before.

He didn't give women control of anything. He didn't give anyone in his life control of anything. Because he always had to be the one.

Always.

But not here. Not with her.

She had him on the edge of exploding. And yet she wouldn't give him relief.

She could feel his mounting desire, and knew exactly when to pull back.

It was pleasure and pain unlike any he had ever known before. He pushed two fingers inside of her as she continued to lick him, and she moaned against his shaft, the vibrations sending sparks of desire through him.

"Let me have you," he growled. "Let me have this," he said, pushing his fingers deeper.

"Not yet," she said.

"I can't give you any more."

"I think you can."

She sucked the head of him into her mouth hard, and he almost lost control then and there. Almost came into her gorgeous mouth.

But the promise of taking her like he wanted to kept him from doing it.

She moved away from him, and lay down like a queen, her head propped up on the pillows, her back arched, her elbows resting on the mattress. "You can have me now. But only if you tell me exactly what I am."

He knew. He knew what he had to say, and he would say anything to get inside of her.

He moved to her, gripped the back of her head and took her mouth in a searing kiss. Then he thrust deep into her wet heat, the relief of being inside of her making him curse. "My wife," he said, the words dragged straight from the center of his chest.

"Yes," she said.

And then finally he was fucking her. Taking her.

It was everything he needed. Everything. And he cried out her name as desire overtook him. She said his in return as she dug her nails into his shoulders, as she gave herself over to her orgasm, her internal muscles milking every last drop out of him.

He had done it. He had surrendered. He had consigned them both to hell.

But they had both gone in together.

So they would have to figure out what this looked like. He had tried to make rules. They had broken them.

They were married, and they'd consummated. There

was no going back. So now they would have to move forward with all of these broken shards.

There was only one answer. At least as far as he could see it. They had to exhaust this. Until it didn't have teeth. Until it didn't own or control them.

Until they could find a way to wear it into something comfortable. And perhaps at that point they would have fucked so much they would have the appetite for someone else.

You will never want anyone but her. You were cursed that day at the pool. And behold the aftereffects of that curse.

And yet, she was in his bed. So perhaps it was only a curse in part.

She snuggled up against him, her hand on his chest. "Mine," she said.

He felt like he couldn't breathe again, but this time he couldn't blame the tightness of his tie.

He had made his bed. And he would use it thoroughly.

CHAPTER TWELVE

THE NEXT MORNING Heather had the feeling she might be staring down wrath and retribution.

So it was a shock to wake up to find a tray of coffee and pastries on her nightstand. She was surprised that he didn't look angry. Standing there, gazing down at her, half dressed and gorgeous. Last night had been intense. And given the way things often were between them, that was saying something.

"Get dressed. We're leaving."

And here it was. The other shoe was about to drop. He was going to distance himself again. Become her forbidding stepbrother, rather than her passionate husband.

"I'm taking you on a honeymoon," he said.

She sat up quickly, letting her blankets fall away. "Excuse me?"

"I am taking you on a honeymoon. I did not stutter."

"You didn't. But that's not anything that we talked about."

"No. But things have changed."

"I have an ultrasound appointment next week."

"I'm aware. We discussed it. But we're going to

go to the Bahamas for a few days. I have a private island there."

"Of course you do. Is that where you take other women?"

The look he gave her was long-suffering. "It is where other people often schedule luxury vacations, but it is mine, and I wish to use it, so I will."

Of course, luxury vacationing was literally his industry. And her first conclusion had been one that let her rest on jealousy. Because it was comfortable, honestly.

"When I think about you with other women it makes me feral," she said, slightly annoyed with herself that she had given him that much. But they were married now. Why should she be embarrassed? Why should she feel insecure? He was hers. The end.

"You're like me," he said, his tone grim.

"In what sense?"

"You already know."

She marinated on that while eating, and on the drive to the airfield. Then further on the plane. She was in love with him. She knew that. She didn't think that he did. Nor did she think that he returned the feelings. For as much as they felt in sync when it came to sex, when she talked to him she still felt like there was a wall up between them.

So whatever commonality he was assuming, she wasn't going to make the same assumption. Not when she could still feel that distance.

"What made you decide on this?" She decided to

ask that rather than continuing to push at something he didn't seem to want to discuss.

"Things have changed. And you and I need to come to a firm agreement on how everything is going to work. When we're back in our lives at the estate, I imagine that will be the time. We have months before the baby is born."

"Are you taking me on a sex vacation?"

His dark eyes sharpened, a muscle in his square jaw leafing upward. "Yes. Do you have a problem with that?"

"Not at all. I just thought I would make sure of what my expectations were. You don't want to bring a knife to a gunfight."

"No indeed." He was silent for a moment.

"I hope you're prepared to do this. You're the one who put us in this situation."

"Oh, because I seduced you?" she asked.

"Yes."

"You folded like a house of cards. Your resistance was futile, and hollow, I might add. No wonder you had to stay away from me."

"We cannot be like this. Because here we are yet again, bringing knives and guns. When we should be endeavoring not to fight," he said.

"I'm actually not trying to fight you. But I am pointing out that if you want to cast blame, you're going to have to have a little bit of honesty. You didn't want to resist this."

"No. But I'm well aware of the potential cost," he said.

"You don't think that we're going to have so much sex this week that we can burn it out of our systems?"

"No. But perhaps it will be less…knife-like."

"What are you afraid of?" she asked.

He raised a dark brow. "I'm not afraid of anything. But I am wary. You and I have been adversaries far longer than we've been lovers. Somehow, we have to find a different way to be."

He wasn't wrong about that. It wasn't all about the baby anymore. It was about them. Their relationship mattered. For the sake of it. Not simply for the sake of somebody else.

"What if we were happy?" she said. "What if we had a lovely relationship, and great sex?"

He laughed, dry. "What a lofty and valiant goal. That is what I would like. But look at the state of the world."

"You're very cynical for a man born into money."

"Only because I know that money doesn't fix every problem. Because I know how toxic people can be with one another regardless."

When they touched down on his island, the first thing that captured her imagination was the blue. The ocean was so clear, so vivid. Even in the deepest parts, as they were descending she could see flying fish as they rose to the surface and glided up out of the water, and then as they moved over the shallows, she could see stingrays floating like underwater birds, slow and peaceful.

The sand was bright white and smooth, the nature pristine and undisturbed.

"The house is stocked for our arrival. All of our meals are prepared. No one will disturb us here."

"Oh."

She got off the plane, and he gestured to a waiting car. He drove them both away from the airfield, and to the center of the island, to the place with the highest elevation, which wasn't much on the relatively flat plain. But they could see over the trees, down to the beach. The house itself was all glass and stone, letting all the beauty of the island in, with no need for privacy, since they were the only inhabitants. The high ceilings had skylights, letting in the warmth from the sun, and probably offering fantastic views of the stars at night.

She drifted from the entryway into the kitchen, which had black stone slab countertops, with a large platter set in the center, filled with sliced and gloriously arranged tropical fruits. "There's no one here?"

"No." He turned and looked behind him, and they could both see the jet they had come in on taking off.

"We are the only people on the entire island."

She nodded, and dropped her purse down to the floor. Then she took off her shirt, her skirt and everything else.

"We don't need clothes then, I guess."

She knew she had him then.

His smile turned wolfish, and whatever reserve he'd been trying to keep was gone entirely now.

"I don't suppose we do."

The days passed in the loveliest haze. Time, status, reality had no meaning. There was no discussion about the future. No attempts at reasoning out what they had between them. They didn't talk about the past. They didn't talk about the future. They were in something like an eternal present, which was definitely different. And lovely in its way.

It also gave her even more of a chance to know him. Just as he was. Not just the difficult things in their past, the way that it related to her. Not the ways in which they had hurt each other and the why. But what he was interested in now. Though she found herself feeling curious about other things. She should let sleeping dogs lie. The sleeping dogs being his past physical relationships. But she felt raw about them. And this felt like a safe space. It wasn't the estate, where so many memories, so many unkind words that had been exchanged between them hung in the air. It wasn't his turf in London, or hers in New York. This was a liminal space where everything seemed just a little bit kinder. They were Adam and Eve here. Unburdened and unashamed.

She was lying out in the white sand, and he was walking out of the crystal clear water, naked. The water glistened on his body, his muscular chest, his thighs— thick and defined, and so sexy she was developing a new fetish. She wouldn't have said that she was into men's thighs. But now she was quite corrected.

"What kinds of relationships have you had?" she asked, staring at him from her lounging place in the sand.

He looked down at her and pushed dark hair off of

his forehead, water droplets flowing down his forearm, through the valleys created by his muscles.

"I don't live in your head, Heather. You are going to have to give me some context."

"I was a virgin," she said. "And yes, some of it was that every time I considered having sex with a man, I imagined you bursting through the door and pulling him off of me. But then at a certain point I just imagined you. It kept me from ever having a sexual relationship. I feel slightly wounded that I didn't have the same impact on you."

He made a dismissive noise, and she bristled.

"Don't look at me like that," he said. "I have no desire to fight with you. By the time I noticed you as a woman, I was no virgin. I was seventeen. And so, I already had experience. Also, I determined that I was never going to touch you."

"You did a bad job at that."

"Yes, thank you. I am aware of that."

"What were your relationships like? Have you ever been in love? It's easy for you to know my history. But I don't know yours. That seems stunningly unfair."

"I'm sorry that it seems unjust to you." He was silent for a moment. And then he sat down beside her in the sand, his proximity taking away some of her irritation. Some of her anger. It was funny how it used to be the opposite. But now that she could touch him when she wanted to, she didn't feel quite so much negative energy around him. She felt close to him. Which was unexpected.

"I knew that I was never going to fall in love," he

said. "And I was always very up-front with my lovers about that. I can have any woman I wanted. Except for you. And I think that might've tempered some of my activity. I might've been a monster otherwise. But there was always tension. The knowledge that there was a woman out there that I wanted more than the one that I was with."

Her stomach went tight. "But you knew you would never fall in love?"

"No. I know that I can't."

"Why not?" Her mouth was dry, her heart sore. Because she loved him. She did. She had. And he was telling her that he couldn't. This man who had captured so much of her for so many years was telling her he had always known he couldn't love. He wanted her. But just a bit more than all those other women. And she supposed that she should be thankful for that? That she should be flattered? But that wasn't the word. No.

Flattered was not the word. "Because I know how it looked on my mother. And I know… It has the capacity to be such a toxic thing. It simply isn't something I would ever willingly subject myself to. Or anyone else. I made a decision a long time ago that I was never going to put anyone through that."

"So they were meaningless to you."

He nodded. "Yes. They were." He looked at her directly. "You don't need to be jealous of women that I've already forgotten."

"How would you feel if I had a long list of ex-lovers?"

He practically bared his teeth. "I would want to

hunt them down and kill them because they had seen you naked."

"Then don't begrudge me my own feelings of being feral over the women that have seen you."

"But no one has shared a bed with me all night. And no one has stayed on a private island with me. And certainly no one else has ever had my baby."

"I'm your wife," she said. Because she couldn't say that she loved him. She just knew she couldn't. Not after this. But she could remind him that she was his wife. That she mattered to him. That what they had was special. Unique. Not like what he had shared with anyone else.

"You are my wife. And it is not enough for us to satisfy each other for an evening. We have to make this work for a lifetime."

Yes. Forever. She didn't need to worry about it. She didn't need to push him. They had forever. He was right. And one thing that she knew about herself and Romeo was that they could hang onto something for more years than most. They had already had this obsession for years. Surely they could continue defeat it. Cultivate it. School it into something better, nicer. "Yes," she said. "We have forever."

They had already made it this far. There was no telling how much further they would be able to make it.

But only if she gave him the time that he needed.

CHAPTER THIRTEEN

THEY HAD TO be back from the honeymoon far too soon
for his liking. But by the time they arrived back at the
estate, he had everything in order. In his mind. There,
the days and nights had been all the same. They had
rarely worn clothes, and if they had it had only been
for the purpose of the joy in removing them. They had
eaten when they felt like it, slept when they felt like
it, fucked when they felt like it. It had been exactly
what he had hoped for. A kind of fresh beginning that
was desperately needed. Without the baggage they carried everywhere else. And so now they were back at
the estate. And he knew exactly how to take all the
things they had created on the honeymoon and make
them work here. They could be friends by day. Lovers
at night. And it would not be the sort of uncontained
passion his parents had had. The turbulence that had
marked his childhood.

No. This would be good.

He wouldn't even have to be as firm as he had imagined. Because everything with her was going so easily. Perhaps they were different people now. Perhaps
this was much more feasible than he had originally

thought. The sharpness might be worn away. A glorious possibility.

This was the first time he had felt entirely calm. Entirely in control. Today was the day they were finding out the sex of the baby. The doctor was coming to the estate, which meant that there was no need for the two of them to prepare to go out. He hadn't expected to feel nervous about this.

"You've seen the baby before?" he asked as she lay down in the bed, wearing her nightgown.

"Yes," she said.

"And everything looks good?"

"Yes. Everything so far has been completely normal."

"I should've been with you."

"We weren't… It's okay."

Except suddenly it felt like it wasn't, and he couldn't readily explain that. At the estate, they did have staff. At the estate, they did live in that glorious bubble of isolation. This house held memories. And for some reason they felt particularly heavy today. Even as the doctor arrived and shook his hand. She was the same doctor that Heather had seen in New York. She had very generously flown over, though he also had a feeling they were paying handsomely for the privilege.

He didn't care. Right then he felt like he would pay anything. As long as everything would go well.

As long as he could make sure that everything would be just fine. That Heather would be safe. That the baby would be safe. Things just felt heavy today.

He felt like something was clawing inside of his

chest, trying to get out. An intensity that he had denied at every other point in his life, except at times when he had taken Heather to bed.

This thing that he had always thought lived inside of him.

The thing that had been confirmed when he had pulled that man off of Heather all those years ago and had nearly committed a murder over it.

He watched as all of the equipment was set up. He wasn't particularly interested in technology, or rather he never had been. Not medical technology. But suddenly, all of these things seemed unbearably important. Because they would measure the health of Heather's pregnancy. Of their child.

"Can you explain to me what everything here does?" he asked, moving in near to the doctor.

Heather laughed. "You're not doing any of it," she said.

"But I could," he said.

"You didn't go to medical school."

"I could figure it out."

"That is the most nonsensical masculine idiocy that I've ever heard. At least, since we negotiated our marriage contract."

He looked over at the doctor, who wasn't saying anything, but silently setting up equipment. "And we worked that out," he said.

"In," she responded noncommittally.

"Okay," the doctor said, turning and smiling. "Heather, this time we just do the Doppler on your stomach. I'm going to do a full anatomy scan, and make sure that everything is looking like it's on track."

"What if it's not?" Romeo asked.

"Wow," Heather said. "That's reassuring."

"What. It's a serious question. What if it isn't?"

"There are certain things that can be fixed now in utero," the doctor responded. "There are heart surgeons who can fix defects before the baby is born. And of course we look for other things. Things that aren't survivable. And we would advise you on the best medical decision, but of course ultimately it's up to you."

With the blankets in bed around her hips, and her nightgown pulled up over her expanding bump, Heather said nothing as the doctor put gel on her stomach and pressed the Doppler against her skin.

"Are you finding out the sex?"

"Yes," they both said.

But then he could think about nothing, because suddenly, there was the baby. And arm, and hand. A profile. He hadn't expected to be able to recognize anything. But he did. There was truly a child growing inside of her. That they had created in a moment of desperation. The kind of heated lust that he had never felt at any other time in his life. The kind he had never felt for anyone else.

And the end result was this. It was miraculous. It grabbed him by the throat and held him hard. She was measuring things. Organs, and though he couldn't ascertain what was normal, he recognized certain things. The child's brain. The heart, fluttering there. He had known that they were having a baby. Of course he had.

It was why they had done all of this. It was why they were together. But he hadn't been able to imagine it. Concrete in a way it hadn't been when it had only been a due date. A rounding of her curves.

"And there," the doctor said. "Right there you can see. That is a baby boy."

"Everything looks good. I don't have any concerns based on this ultrasound. And I would say that your due date is right on."

"Oh," Heather said. "We both know exactly when the baby was conceived."

"Not everyone does."

"Indeed not," Romeo said. He smiled, and tried to look filled with good humor, but there was something about this that was sitting like a weight on his chest. A son. He was having a son.

And look at how the relationship with his own father had been. Their father-and-son bond had been severed forever by Romeo's inability to come to grips with his feelings. His father had died without Romeo ever reconciling with him. He had never... He had never managed to fix it. Because the truth was, all the toxicity that he had seen between his parents lived inside of him. Either learned or inherited, he didn't know. Heather's mother had been...

It seemed as if she loved in a superior fashion. Certainly she had loved his father in a way that his father had not been able to love Carla. In a way that his father had not been able to love Romeo. And in a way Romeo had certainly never managed to demonstrate affection.

All he knew was great and terrible pain. All he knew was all-consuming, desperate, painful.

And what would he do with this boy? He would need every ounce of strength and willpower. He would need… He would need greatly to expand his emotional bandwidth, which currently felt all taken up.

"Are you okay?" Heather asked after she had gotten out of bed, the doctor still taking the equipment and preparing it for transport again.

"Yes. Did you want to go and shop for the nursery?"

"Yes," she said. "I very much do."

"There is a shop in town that sells lovely, locally made furniture. Perhaps we can go to the village."

"I would love that. It's been so long since I've actually left the estate and spent any time here."

She was looking at him like he was losing it, which was maybe fair. Maybe fair since he felt like he was coming apart inside. Even if there was no reason.

They took one of his father's classic cars down to the village, and Heather stroked the dashboard. "He loved this."

"He did," Romeo said, his throat tightening. God. He hadn't anticipated this. Hadn't anticipated that there would be such a host of regrets connected to his own father as he faced down this new iteration of a father-son relationship. What had he thought? Of course there was always going to be a chance that it would be a son. He hadn't thought that it would matter. Maybe it didn't. Maybe he would feel equally unable to parent a daughter. But this felt like the potential to be a mirror. And he didn't want to repeat the same steps that he had already walked with his father, only backward.

No. The very idea was punishing.

The village itself was charming. It always had been, though Romeo himself had never spent an immense amount of time there. His mother had always taken him with her when she had traveled. She had required him to be her emotional support, she had always said. Even when his parents had been married, when she had gone on location for photo shoots, she had always taken him. His youth had been nomadic, or it had been stagnant. Because when they were at the estate, generally, whatever was happening was between his parents. And not him.

He had only been cannon fodder.

He swallowed hard, trying to regain his focus. This was about his child. This was about Heather.

"Romeo, you don't seem okay," she said.

"I'm fine," he growled. He was searching the narrow streets for a place to park, and nearly cursing everything before finding a place near the store that he was looking for.

They got out, and walked down the old, crooked lane into a stone building that housed handmade furniture made by local artisans.

And Heather was immediately bright and cheery and looking at rocking chairs, cradles and cribs. Toy boxes. So he was trying to pull himself out of the funk that he found himself in, because she was enjoying this. She'd—

His phone rang.

His mother.

He sighed, trying to disperse the tension in his chest.

It didn't work.

Predictably.

"Yes?"

"You haven't called me," she said.

"I'm sorry. I've been busy. I was on honeymoon, and now Heather and I have just found out that we're having a son."

She did not congratulate him. Because she wasn't in the headspace. He had known that the minute he had seen her name on his phone, and he didn't even know why he was bothering to introduce it into the conversation.

"I need you to come back to Vienna."

"I can't," he said.

"Romeo," his mother said, her tone shocked. "I'm not feeling well. I'm afraid… What if I hurt myself?"

"Mother," he said. "You have a therapist. And I need you to follow the instructions that he's given you. If you really feel as if you're in danger, then you need to check yourself into the hospital. You know that I can't get there immediately anyway. But I'm shopping. For furniture for my child."

"The baby isn't even born yet."

"No, but he will be," Romeo said, a cold rage filling his chest. His mother. His fragile mother, who didn't do this on purpose, and he knew that. But suddenly everything just felt wrong. It felt angry. It felt awful.

Suddenly, everything felt like it was in danger of breaking apart.

Because his entire childhood had been fucked. And if he wasn't able to build walls around all of this, then it was only going to be the same. He wanted his mother to be in his son's life. But he would not allow his son to give endlessly to his grandmother. Not when she was supposed to give to him. And that's how it would be. If ever Romeo did not have the energy, she would try to bypass him and get his child. It was what she had done to him. When she couldn't get attention from his father she had…

"I love you," Romeo said. "You know that. But I have a family. And—"

"This is about your wife. Because of course you care about her more than you do me. Because of course, she's just like her mother and—"

"Mother," Romeo said. "This is only you trying to make a bad feeling inside of you worse. Because if you do that, then you know that you can get me on a plane."

"Are you accusing me of manipulating you?"

"Yes. Whether you're doing it on purpose or not. Heather and I will come visit you soon. But I need you to follow your plan. I need you to take care of yourself. Because I have to take care of my family."

Anger was threatening to tear a hole through his chest. He couldn't act on it. He couldn't treat his mother the way that his father did. That would be awful. It would be inexcusable. There would be no justification for it. None whatsoever.

Why did his feelings feel like they were going to choke him out?

He had to get a grip on them. He had to get a grip

on himself. This was the kind of life he did not want his child living.

Whether it be from his mother, whether it be from him. Because it lived in him. It was threatening to get out now, to burn everything to the ground. To take everything that he had ever tried to do with his mother and render it useless.

Because part of him wanted to tell her to just do it already if she was going to.

It was years of anger and exhaustion, and he knew that he couldn't say that. He knew he couldn't.

"Call your doctor."

He hung up the phone, and looked across the store at Heather. As she began to make her way toward him as he picked up his phone and called his mother's therapist. "I need you to do a check-in on my mother. Please go to the house as quickly as you can. She's supposed to call you. But I don't necessarily trust that she will."

Heather frowned. As soon as he hung the phone up she spoke. "What's going on?"

"My mother is being my mother. Nothing out of the ordinary."

He was trying to make light of it. Trying not to let her see the dark mess that his soul was in.

"I have some favorites. But only if you like them."

"No. This is… You can choose."

He followed her through the store, with one goal in mind. To keep everything together. He had to keep everything together. This was what he had proposed. He and Heather would be friends. During the day. They would not give in to the toxic side of their relationship. They wouldn't surrender to it.

He repeated that. As she chose furniture and made arrangements to have it delivered. As they went and bought blankets. Baby clothes. As she handed him a tiny white onesie that seemed impossibly small. Didn't seem like it could possibly contain a real human. Much less one that he was going to have to take care of. But he was desperate. He was desperate for it to be night. Because he needed her. He needed to exhaust the demons inside of him. He needed to do something.

He needed to make sure that she never saw this. He needed to make sure that he was never his own mother. That he didn't vent his toxicity onto other people.

In the bedroom. That was where he could release this.

It was the only safe place.

CHAPTER FOURTEEN

SHE COULD SENSE the change in him. He was pretending that nothing was wrong, and it was baffling her. He had experienced a near personality switch after they had found out that the baby was going to be a boy, and then his mother had called him, and he had refused to give her any details about it. But he was obviously upset. But also not flying to Vienna.

She had the chef at the estate make them a celebratory meal. She was happy they were having a boy. She would've been happy with anything, of course, but it was the way that it felt more real now. The way that she felt like she could actually picture their child.

A little boy like Romeo.

It made her heart ache. She loved them both so much. She loved this vision of their future. But the distance between herself and her husband felt…awful.

That was the thing that scared her the most.

But he was becoming more withdrawn, and the later that it got, the more pronounced that became. He practically didn't speak during their meal. And when they were finished they began to walk toward the bedroom they were sharing, and as soon as the door closed, he kissed her. Hard and punishing. This was Romeo as he had been months ago. The man who had taken her like he was possessed.

This was how he had been on their wedding night. Something was wrong. This wasn't gentle.

This was something else. Possessive, intense. Angry.

"Romeo," she said.

"Heather," he responded, wrapping her hair around his hand and pulling her head back, kissing her neck, her throat, down to her collarbone.

She gasped. Because even though she felt like there was something wrong, she was a slave to this. A slave to him. To the intensity of the desire between them. It was too good.

He looked up at her, something haunted in his dark eyes, and then he grabbed the edges of her blouse and tore it open, exposing her breasts. She hadn't worn a bra today, because everything was ill fitting and she hadn't had a chance to get something more comfortable. And judging by the light in his eyes, he appreciated that.

"That's what I thought. I was staring at your breasts, trying to see if you had anything underneath. I thought that I saw your nipples get tight anytime I got near you. You want me," he said, desperation carving an edge into his voice.

"Of course I do. I've always wanted you."

"It's a sickness. For you just like it is for me."

She gripped his face, and stared into his eyes. "It's not a sickness. It's the best thing that's ever happened to me."

He growled, like a wounded beast, and pressed his hand between her shoulder blades, arching her back toward him and lowering his head so that he could suck a nipple deep into his mouth. It was nearly violent, the edge to his desire gloriously unhinged. And she was caught between the desire to soften it and to push them further. To reassure him, or to give him a place where he could have whatever he needed.

She realized it wasn't one or the other. It was like they had been trying to make it one or the other. All this time.

Their days were soft, their nights filled with passion. But she wanted to get back to their honeymoon. Where every moment had been both.

And he seemed desperate to draw all these lines.

She knew why. It was clear that everything with his parents was painful. Complicated. It was clear that it had created a situation where something about emotional intimacy terrified him. She didn't fully understand. But she wanted to. And if this was the doorway, then she had to let him open it like this. If this was what he needed, then she needed to let them have it. Needed to let it go all the way, because somehow she had a feeling that on the other side of it she would find that way to him. That perhaps this would demolish the wall just enough for her to climb over.

Or maybe she just wanted him. All of him. His good, his ugly. His hard and his soft. His rough and his tender. She certainly didn't want it from anyone else.

She was incapable of it. He forced her down onto her knees, and she trembled as he undid his belt. There was a place for making him beg. But there was a place for her to beg as well, and she knew that this was the moment.

"Please," she said. "Let me have you."

"You want this," he said, gripping himself at the base and bringing his hardness to her lips.

"Yes," she said. "I do."

"Even when I'm like this?"

"Especially when you're like this."

He pushed his way into her mouth, and began to thrust hard against the back of her throat. Every moment that they'd resisted was leading to this. Not to that first time, but to this moment.

He was pushing her. He was testing her, and she was going to pass. She was going to do more than pass. Because she didn't just tolerate this. She loved it. She wanted it all.

He wasn't too powerful for her. If anything, she was too powerful for him, and this moment was proving it.

Because he was at the end of himself, and he needed her. Needed her strength. Needed her touch.

She could be there for him. She would.

He pulled her mouth away, and brought her back up to her feet, kissing her, deep and hard and bruising. She gasped as he reached around and cupped her ass, squeezing her tight before turning her away from him, wrapping her hair around his hand again as he bent her over the bed. "Ask for it," he said.

"Please," she said. "Please take me."

He thrust into her from behind, one hand on her hip,

the other holding her hair fast as he lost himself inside of her. As he pushed them both to the brink.

This was what he needed.

This was what they both needed.

He released her hair, reached around and gripped her chin, held her face and turned it back toward him as he leaned down to kiss her, violently as he continued to thrust inside of her. Like he was reminding himself of who he was with. As if he needed the reminder.

"Romeo," she said, saying his name because she knew that it would undo him. Because she knew that however much he was more powerful than her physically, she had a different power altogether.

He growled, leaned down and bit her shoulder as he thrust hard into her one last time, coming hard as he pushed her right over with him. He rested his forehead against her back, and she could feel the sweat on his brow. Could feel all of his intensity. All of his anger. Everything.

She turned, uncoupling with him and kissing him deep on his lips, moving her hands through his hair. "I love you," she whispered against his mouth.

His whole body shivered.

"I do," she whispered. "I love you. Do you know how much? That's why we can be friends. That's why we can be friends and we can be this. We can be both and everything."

He pressed his forehead against the curve of her neck. "My mother had another episode today."

"And you didn't fly to Vienna?"

"No. I didn't. Because today had to be about our child. Because everything has to be about our child."

"I don't agree," she said. "I'm glad that you did that. But I hope that you did it for you. Because you're allowed to live, Romeo. Your life matters apart from her. It just does. And you shouldn't be made to feel like you have to drop everything to give her whatever she needs."

"You understand. It's me. I'm not any different from her."

"You're very different from her. You are not fragile."

"No. I'm angry. So is she, and she has mental illness on top of it, so the way that she chooses to express it is different. The way that she is able to express it is different. But I am petty, and I am vindictive. Look at the way that I treated you all throughout school."

"We were young. And you were going through things."

"Yes. It's true. I was. But I don't know another way to be. And that is the honest truth. I do not know another way. And I know what it's like to be held hostage by someone whose emotions are… It's her. I did to my own father, after all."

"You were a teenage boy. We spoke about this already. Your father should've reconciled things between the two of you."

"Maybe. But I was also prepared to hold him at arm's length forever. Punishment. I cannot believe that version of myself. I will not be what my mother has been to our child. I will not be that to you. Every strong emotion I have turned sour. And I will not sub-ject you to that."

"Maybe you should ask me what I want to be sub-jected to. Maybe you don't get to make all the deci-sions."

"It isn't about controlling you. It's about controlling myself. And I… You will fall out of love with me. This I guarantee you."

"No," she said. "I won't."

Pain tore at her chest. Because she wanted to stay with him forever. She really did. They had a whole agreement. And suddenly, the agreement didn't matter anymore. Because it wasn't about a set of ideal circum-stances that they were creating for their baby. It was about what the two of them could have. And what he wasn't allowing because he was so afraid.

But she couldn't carry on like that. So she was going to have to make this into something he couldn't con-trol. Because that's what he was trying to do. She un-derstood now. He was just so afraid of the strength of all of this. So he was trying to separate things. His mother, her, their passion versus their friendship. And this reality of having a child was what had pushed him over the edge. It was what had made it all too much.

She could understand that. She could sympathize with him. But she couldn't enable it. She simply couldn't. Not when they could have everything. And if he was going to draw lines so that he could hide be-hind them, so that he could give them both the least of what they could have, then she wasn't going to be complicit in that.

Because what he didn't understand was that there were other ways to hurt people.

"I love you. I love you enough to try and take a risk now. I love... Romeo. We've been fighting this fight for so many years. Fighting to stay away from each other. And we lost that, didn't we? So now, I want to fight to have the most of what we can have. I think we were meant to be together. Maybe we're the love story. Have you ever thought of that? Maybe all of this happened so that you and I could be together. Maybe we're the happy ending."

"I believe that's true," he said. "We are a mess. Created by a mess. And I believe that we can do our best with it, but I can't—"

"You're afraid. Then I understand that. Your mother turned love into a weapon for years. She turned it into a task that you had to complete. And today you did something incredible. You chose a different path. It doesn't change how much you love her. If she tries to make you feel differently, then that's on her. It's not you. Your love is the same. Whether or not we call what we have love, it's the same. I love you, and I think that you love me. But I don't want to have friendship and sex. When I decided to marry you, I decided that I was doing it because I wanted you. In the beginning, it was about the baby. But that's just a story I was telling myself. In the end, it's about you and me. It's about our love story."

"You don't understand what you're asking for."

"I do. I'm asking for you. All of you. And what part of me has ever seemed like I couldn't handle all of you?

It's been that way from the beginning. When we only knew how to hurt each other."

"Maybe that's all I ever know how to do. Maybe that's the most that it will ever be."

"No. I just don't believe it. I'm sorry. I know that it might make you feel better to think that this is all we have, because you want something to numb it, don't you? You want some kind of a break from all of this. But this is intense, I fear. Becoming parents. Being married. Being in love."

"And what exactly are you proposing?"

"The agreement is out the window. You're going to have to penalize me. I'll give you everything. Every penny that I have. But we will have to figure out how to coparent. Because I'm not scared anymore. What I'm scared of is us having only a little when we can have everything. That's what I'm scared of. And that's what I won't allow."

"You can't leave me," he said.

"I can. And if you love me, you'll follow me. But if you don't you let me go. And I will never keep you out of your child's life. I'm sorry for what I said when I first found out that I was pregnant. But I would never do that to you. Not now. Not now that I know you. But I know you well enough to take this risk. So I'm giving you one more chance. Do you think you can ever love me?"

She saw fear in his eyes. Real. Raw.

"No."

"Then I can't stay with you."

He said nothing while she packed her things and

left. There was nothing to say. She had said it all. She wanted something that he did not have the ability to give, and he had no choice but to let her go. It was the only kind thing. It was the only thing he could do. She wanted to escape him, so he needed to let her do it. There was no other option.

But as soon as she was gone, he began the process of tearing everything apart. Absolutely everything. The bedroom, and then he went down the hall and went into the room he lived in so infrequently as a child.

And he began to dismantle that as well. There could be nothing left. None of these false promises. None of this...

The pain inside of him was like a living thing. It had teeth. Monstrous teeth.

He was undone. He was finished. Because if he didn't have Heather, what did he have?

It was like years' and years' worth of pain was pushing forward now. It was like all of the feelings that he had ever withheld from himself were crashing in on him now.

Years of it.

Why was his mother not like other mothers?

Why did his father care more about her, and then his new wife? His new stepdaughter? Why never him?

Why did he always have to work to have love? Why did he always have to give? Until he had nothing left. Nothing for his father, who he had shut out, and then there was her.

Then there was her.

He could remember when she had first appeared,

and it was like a demon had risen up inside of him and told him that he had no choice but to deny her. He had to.

And then, when he was seventeen, it had become clear why.

Her beauty intoxicated him. His desire for her surpassed any desire he had ever felt for any other woman. And it made him mean. It made him want to lash out at her. It made him want to push her away.

Because she was the key to unlocking the door that he kept so carefully locked.

The one that kept him from being his father or his mother.

The one that kept him safe.

Always.

He gazed around the room, at all the destruction.

He had torn apart the bed. He had put holes in the wall.

He was like an animal. He had always known he would be.

Confirmed when he had first seen Heather with that other man.

Oh God. It had been confirmed then. Because he had been tempted to rip that fool's head off. He was lucky that he hadn't.

So very lucky.

He had been fighting this all those years. That his feelings for her were too strong. That they were...

That they were in love. And for him that was toxic, and it always would be.

She wanted them to have everything? He couldn't have everything. He couldn't.

And how did she leave him? How dare she. When he had been trying to save her.

You were trying to save yourself.

Maybe.

But he feared the alternative would be to drown.

CHAPTER FIFTEEN

SHE DIDN'T GO to New York. Instead, she went to London. She went to Catherine.

"Oh, my friend," Catherine said, pulling her in for a hug.

"I'm pathetic," she said.

"You're not pathetic. Well. You are a little bit. Tell me what happened."

"I demanded his love. And when he refused to give it to me I left him. Because I believe that he does love me. And I'm sort of just playing chicken with his fear now."

"Well. It was strong of you."

"What if he doesn't love me? What if he doesn't come after me?"

Catherine sighed, and brought her into the kitchen, where she immediately began to heat up the electric kettle. "Oh, he will come after you, my dear. The question is only in what capacity he will do it. Because he is not a soft man. Which means he's going to chase you down."

"He didn't. He just let me leave."

"Well. That means he's more scared of you than you are of him."

"But I don't understand… I don't understand how. I don't understand why it's so scary to him."

"It's scary to you too. But also he's a man, so it's going to take him longer to get there."

"But I was brave."

"Because women are. Think of everything your mom went through, and she still fell in love with your stepdad. Not just because it was advantageous to her. She really fell in love with him. And think about what Romeo put you through, but you still have a greater understanding of what your actual feelings are than he does. Honestly. Men have greater physical strength, but we…we have stronger hearts. And we have to, because if we didn't, why would we keep falling in love with those creatures?"

"I'm being selfish. I could let them be comfortable. But then I wouldn't be. And I just don't think we can thrive that way. I really don't. I think it would explode eventually, and it would be a mystery as to why. But I see it now. I see it clearly. I know why. Because if he keeps building walls, I'm going to keep trying to push them down. And he will resist harder, and… We can't keep doing that."

"No. But of course the man is going to want to see his baby."

"Of course. And I want him to see his baby. I've never said otherwise. But…my mother lived for me. For years. I'm grateful. We were all happier when she began to live as a whole person. Well, except Romeo.

All of this is such a sore subject for him, and I think it's difficult for him to talk about, or maybe even understand."

"You tried. And in the end, if that's the best you've got, then it's the best you've got. You tried."

It was a lovely sentiment. She thought about it while she went to sleep in Catherine's guest room. But she didn't want to try and fail. She loved Romeo Accardi. With everything she had in her. And if after all this time, all this pain, all this pleasure, they couldn't find a way to call it what it was, then she had failed.

She was strong. And she would go on. She would be the best mother to her son.

But part of herself would be lost. The part of herself that had fallen in love with Romeo all those years ago.

He was going out of his mind. She wasn't there. He had gone all the way to New York to find her, had gone to her penthouse, and discovered that she wasn't there.

It made him want to tear apart her home, but even he had limits. It made him want to lash out, at everyone. And everything.

This was love for him, unchecked. Painful. This was him. The absolute truth of who he was. And he despised himself.

He stopped right where he was standing, in her living room. And for a heartbeat he was silent. He was still.

And instead of fighting the feeling, instead of lashing out at everything around him, he let it roll over him.

This feeling that he had been running from all of his life.

Love.

He could remember the first time he realized that love had a cost. The first time that in order to get his mother's attention he had to make her feel better. The first time he had heard his father say cruel things when his mother was in the middle of a meltdown. Oh, Giuseppe had not been able to be there for her. He had been cruel in her lowest moments, and that had always made everything feel complicated. Because sometimes Romeo felt that same cruelty, but he would never say it.

He believed in his heart that his father was a good man. But a complicated one. As his mother was a good woman, but a complicated one. And so it wasn't as easy as saying that love the way they expressed it wasn't real. It was the most real love that they were capable of with one another. And with him.

And what real love was Romeo capable of?

You have loved her without exhaustion for years.

Yes. His mother. He had always been willing to do what he had to in order to make her feel safe. Even if it compromised his own happiness. He had not been sacrificial with his father. But maybe it was because he judged him. Because he felt like his father should be able to handle what Romeo had taken on. And then there was Heather. It had always been her. She had always been the only one. The only one who had engaged more than just his body. But his heart.

And he had rewritten that. Had told himself that it was hatred. With the fire of a thousand suns, so that he wouldn't have to…live with the extraordinary, magical, devastating miracle of love.

He knew how strong love was. How complicated.

But when he looked back over the years with her, he didn't feel exhausted. He felt foolish. Because how could he have ever believed that he hated her? He felt small, because he had taken his own fear and fashioned it into a weapon used to keep her away.

But it hadn't worked. Maybe she was right.

There were all these complicated loves. But maybe theirs wasn't. Maybe theirs was the one that was meant to be. Maybe theirs was the one that was stronger than anything else. Maybe theirs was the one that would actually heal, and not hurt.

Because God knew a life without her wouldn't do a damn thing to fix him. But he had to stop running. He had to stop fighting.

He had to stand there, and let in the light.

Eventually she would go back to New York. Eventually she was going to have to tell him where she was. But not right now. Right now she was happy to just live with her best friend and try to piece together some semblance of a routine. She could feel the baby move now. She was so happy about it. And so mad at Romeo that she couldn't share it with him.

She had gone grocery shopping so that she could cook tonight. Something to make her feel alive.

Someday she would inhabit her strength fully. It was not this day. The streetlights were beginning to come on, and she simply couldn't make herself walk faster as she approached Catherine's town house. And then, beneath the glow of the light, she saw a tall, imposing figure. All in black. A man that she would know anywhere. A man that she knew better than anyone else.

"'Wherefore art thou, Romeo?'"

He stepped into the light fully. "I haven't had any poison."

"I'm thankful for that." Her chest tightened. "Why are you here? Because if it's for your wounded pride, to enforce a document or to try and have your way I—"

"It's not. It's not I… I came for you. Not because we signed papers. Not because of my pride. Because of my heart. It would've been so much easier if I could have believed that what my parents had wasn't love. The problem is, it was. My father loved me. My mother loves me. Their best version of love left me scarred. And the intensity of my own feelings…it terrified me. That if I ever love somebody I would hurt them, the same way that my parents hurt each other. That I would hurt a child the same way my mother hurt me. When I met you, it felt like it was confirmed. All of the feelings that we have traded back and forth, it seemed to confirm that. That I would be a danger to you. To me. I kept renegotiating the boundaries, because I wanted you. It isn't going away. It isn't going to change. So I surrender, Heather. To you. To this. To love. If this is how I die, then it's how I die. By loving you. And I would rather experience it that way than to live all the years ever without you."

She didn't have words. So she just stretched up on

her toes and threw her arms around his neck, her grocery bags hitting him in the back. "I love you."

"I love you."

"It won't be the death of us," she whispered.

"How do you know?"

"Because it has kept us going all this time. Even when we called it something else. So let's have this now. Let's have each other. I love you. I love you so much it hurts. And I love that it does. Because it also brings me joy. And so do you."

"Heather... I'm not worthy of that."

"You never had to be. You simply had to be you. That's all it's ever been. It was you from the beginning. And you all the days after."

"And it will be us forever."

She stretched up on her toes and kissed him. She kissed him with all of the love in her body. "Do you know that love has a flavor?"

"What is it?"

"It's you."

EPILOGUE

THEIR LOVE WASN'T painful. It was beautiful. The pain had been in trying to keep it from flourishing. Growth that was being suppressed by fear. But once it was given free rein, it spread over everything. And it made their life beautiful.

Once he let go of the idea that he had to earn everything, even his relationship with his mother improved. And ten years later, as they brought their four children to visit their grandmother for Christmas, going to the house in Vienna felt light. Which was something Romeo would have said was impossible. But it turned out that nothing was truly impossible with love. Especially not the kind like he and Heather had.

They enjoyed a lovely Christmas dinner with Carla, and then went back to their favorite hotel, with all the kids in tow. Though they did complain about having to share a room, since the suite only contained two bedrooms.

"It will build character," Romeo said to his oldest son before he closed the doors and then went to the room where his wife was waiting.

"They're such menaces," she said.

"My favorite ones," he agreed.

He looked at her, and familiar desire stirred in his veins. It had never stopped. This. The profound, glorious ache that he felt for this woman.

This woman who he loved so softly and fiercely. And who he made love with with all the passion contained in his being.

"I have loved you for well over half my life."

"It's true," she said. "Though you would never have called that love back then."

"No. But I was a fool then."

"Were you?"

"Yes." He wrapped his arms around her. "I used to think that hating you had become a habit. But it was just being obsessed with you. Thinking about you. Wanting you."

"What do you think now?"

"Loving you is not a habit, Heather Accardi. It is who I am."

* * * * *

Get up to 4 Free Books!

We'll send you 2 free books from each series you try PLUS a free Mystery Gift.

Both the **Harlequin Presents** and **Harlequin Medical Romance** series feature exciting stories of passion and drama.